ECHO IN THE VALLEY

After four years' separation, Alison had
been forced to return to her husband
Dirk—but only for the sake of her little
boy. Yet why did Dirk want her back
anyway, when he might just as well
have married Yvette Paulson?

ECHO IN THE VALLEY

BY

YVONNE WHITTAL

MILLS & BOON LIMITED
15–16 BROOK'S MEWS
LONDON W1A 1DR

First published 1984
Australian copyright 1984
Philippine copyright 1984
This edition 1984

© Yvonne Whittal 1984

ISBN 0 263 74717 4

Set in Monophoto Plantin 10 on 10½ pt.
01–0884 – 57858

Made and printed in Great Britain by
Richard Clay (The Chaucer Press) Ltd,
Bungay, Suffolk

CHAPTER ONE

ALISON was aware of the anxious thudding of her heart as Dr Leonard Samuels stepped away from the examination table on which her three-year-old son lay stripped to the waist. The doctor's bushy eyebrows met in an ominous frown as he gestured that the nurse should dress the child and, taking Alison's arm, he marched her out of the examination room into the adjoining office and closed the interleading door so that their conversation would not be overhead. Alison squared her shoulders as she faced him, but her delicate features were pale and pinched. Her long, dark brown hair was thick and lustrous, and held away from her face with a tortoiseshell comb, but, trapped in the shaft of sunlight coming through the open window, there was an unexpected hint of copper in its sheen. Her mouth was full, betraying her sensitivity, and her small nose had an attractive upward tilt at the tip. Grey-green eyes were fringed with sweeping dark lashes beneath curved eyebrows, but at that moment her eyes were a bleak grey rather than green.

'What is it, Dr Samuels?' she prompted, and her faintly husky voice sounded even bleaker.

She knew Dr Samuels too well not to recognise the gravity in his manner. He had brought Ferdie into this world, and her little boy's asthmatic ailment had, over the past two years, resulted in many visits to these very consulting-rooms.

'Ferdie isn't getting any better, Alison,' he confirmed her own suspicions, 'and you don't need *me* to tell you that these asthmatic attacks have become more frequent over the past months.'

A coldness invaded her weary body. Dr Samuels

spoke the truth, for she had lost count of the many nights she had sat next to Ferdie's bed in an attempt to ease his breathing with the medication which had been prescribed, and her maternal instincts had warned long ago that this situation could not be allowed to continue indefinitely.

Alison's trembling fingers tightened on the strap of her handbag. 'What am I going to do?'

'There's only one thing you *can* do, as I see it,' the doctor advised grimly. 'Get him away from the coast, and go inland with him.'

'For a holiday, you mean?' she asked hopefully, mentally evading the only obvious solution.

'I mean *permanently*,' he put her fears into words for her. 'Ferdie will eventually outgrow his asthma, I'm certain of that, but not while you remain here in Cape Town.'

'I can't simply give up my job and move away,' she protested against all common sense, and Leonard Samuels' hand gripped her shoulder, his touch conveying the urgency of the situation.

'I know you've worked like a demon to support yourself and the child, and I realise that you've only just begun to reap the rewards of all your hard work, but if you value your child's health, Alison, then you will pack up right now and get him away from the coast.'

'It's as serious as all that?' she heard herself query something which had been staring her in the face for quite some time, and the doctor nodded gravely.

They halted their conversation abruptly when the interleading door opened and a dark-haired little boy stepped into the office with the nurse in tow. Alison's rigid features relaxed, and a smile of tender warmth curved her mouth and lit her eyes as she looked down at her son. He was at the centre of everything she did; he was her reason for living and working so hard, and she dared not risk losing him.

'Let's go home, Ferdie,' she said as he slipped his warm, trusting little hand into hers.

'If you need me you know you only have to call and I'll come,' Leonard Samuels murmured, opening the door for them, and Alison smiled up at him gratefully.

'Thank you, Dr Samuels.'

Ferdie chattered incessantly as they took the lift down to the ground floor of the building and stepped out into the warm autumn sunshine, but Alison barely heard him on this occasion. Her mind was in a turmoil as she attempted to reconcile herself with the inevitable, and it was only when Ferdie sat beside her in her small Renault that she realised he had fallen silent to study her rigidly controlled features.

'Mummy, why are you cross?' he demanded in his unnaturally husky voice, and his grey eyes were wide and searchingly intent on her face.

She heard the faint rattling in his chest as he breathed, but she veiled the deep concern in her eyes and shook her head. 'I'm not cross, darling.'

'You look cross,' he insisted poutingly.

'Oh, Ferdie,' Alison sighed with a catch in her voice and, perilously close to tears, she scooped him into her arms and held him tightly against her. His hands became entangled in her hair, tugging painfully at her scalp as he locked his arms about her neck, but she did not mind the pain at that moment as she held his small, thin body in her arms while she fought hard against the tears which stung her eyelids. 'Let's go home,' she suggested at length when she had managed to control herself. 'I'll warm some milk for you, and you can have some of those biscuits I baked last night.'

'Can I have the biscuits with the nuts in?' he wanted to know as he wriggled out of her arms and allowed her to strap him into the seat.

'You can have whichever ones you want, darling,' Alison smiled shakily, turning the key in the ignition, and neither of them spoke during the drive out to her flat in the northern suburbs.

Alison did not dare pause during the remainder of that afternoon to contemplate the future, and she put up a bright front for Ferdie's sake. Her thoughts could not be curbed, however, when she put him to bed that evening and sat watching his eyelids droop sleepily until his lashes fanned his pale cheeks. Her fingers tenderly brushed a dark curl away from his forehead, but he was asleep and did not stir and, as always, there was that sharp stab of pain when she studied his features reflectively. Ferdie was the image of his father, and no one in their right mind could ever doubt that he was the young son of Dirk du Bois. He had the same raven black hair and grey eyes, and Alison felt certain that his boyish features would one day harden into a replica of his father's rugged good looks.

She sighed heavily and switched off the bedside light, but she sat there a moment longer in the darkness listening to Ferdie's breathing before she rose quietly to her feet and walked out of the room to go and make herself a cup of coffee. When at last she sat down in the lounge with her coffee on the low table beside her, she found herself thinking about the past instead of the future. She had been orphaned at the age of seven, and this had resulted in her being sent from one foster home to another. When, at the age of eighteen, she had completed her education, she discovered that her parents had left her a small legacy which had at least been sufficient to pay her fees for the two years she attended the secretarial college. Alison had been forced to work weekends and holidays to earn a little extra money and, at the age of twenty, when she had graduated from the college, she found that her careful administration of her limited funds had left her with a small but reasonable amount of money in her savings account at the bank. She had bought herself a dilapidated old Austin for next to nothing and taken herself off on a well-deserved holiday into the fascinating winelands of the Cape.

It was in the Berg river valley, close to Paarl, that Alison had first met Dirk du Bois. The Austin's fan-belt had snapped, and she had been staring helplessly at the damage when a jeep turned off the road and stopped a little distance from her. An enormous hulk of a man had emerged from behind the driver's seat to come striding towards her, and from that very moment he had seemed to threaten her very existence. Ruggedly handsome, his piercing grey eyes had raked her small slenderness from head to foot to make her feel as if she had been dissected physically, and her insides had quivered with something close to fear at the raw masculinity he had exuded.

'Dirk du Bois,' he had introduced himself abruptly, his large, rough hand engulfing hers briefly before he turned to examine the fault beneath the Austin's raised bonnet. After assessing the damage his gaze had shifted to her slim ankles and shapely calves while the playful breeze lifted the hem of her dress embarrassingly higher about her legs. 'You're not wearing stockings.'

'N-No,' she had stammered foolishly, blushing under his scrutiny and wondering if she had committed some sort of crime by venturing bare-legged into the valley.

'Do you have a pair somewhere?'

'In my suitcase, yes.'

'Get it.'

Bewildered, she had obeyed him, and fifteen minutes later, with a brand new stocking acting as a temporary fan-belt, she had driven the rest of the way into Paarl with Dirk following her closely in his jeep.

Thinking back, Alison realised that Dirk had simply taken charge of her life from that very day. She had been given accommodation with friends of his in Paarl, and during the following three weeks his overpowering advances had broken through her fragile wall of resistance. He was a man who was accustomed to getting whatever he wanted, and he had made no secret of the fact that he had wanted *her*. Innocent as she might have been, she had also sensed that Dirk was a man who knew more about women than she, at that time, knew about the alien emotions he had begun to arouse in her, and his virile masculinity had been to her more potent than the wine he made and sold under the Bordeaux label on his estate. It was inevitable that she should fall in love with him; madly and irrevocably in love, and she had married him within a month of meeting him.

The incidents which had occurred during those brief months of marriage did not bear thinking about, and Alison shied away from it mentally. She had to think of the future; Ferdie's future and her own. She had to take him away from the coast, and the only place she could think of was that lush valley where the air still smelled sweet and fresh. She could not go to Paarl. *Never* Paarl! She would find a place for Ferdie and herself in Stellenbosch. That was far enough inland, and yet close enough to Cape Town if Ferdie should need to be taken to Dr Samuels for a medical examination.

She wrote out her resignation that evening. There was no point in wasting time, but she found that it was one of the most difficult letters she had ever had to write. Over the past three years she had worked herself up from junior typist to private secretary to one of the directors of the engineering company. They had been good to her, and now she could not help feeling that she would be letting them down, but there was nothing else she could do in the circumstances. Her child's health was more important to her at that moment, and her chin was set with determination when she slipped her letter of resignation into an envelope and sealed it.

Alison dropped Ferdie off at the nursery school on her way to work the following morning. It was a familiar routine, but on this particular morning she felt heavy-hearted. She arrived at her office a few minutes before her employer which gave her time to leave her letter of resignation on his desk blotter where she knew he would find it the moment he arrived, and when she was summoned to his office a half hour later she did not have to guess at the reason for this confrontation.

Arthur Rennie seemed to scowl into his grey beard as he faced her across the width of his desk, and he jabbed a finger agitatedly at her briefly worded letter. 'What's this, Alison? Haven't we been treating you well?'

'It's nothing like that at all, Mr Rennie, and I'm truly sorry,' she began apologetically, 'but I've been told that I must move away from the coast with my son for the sake of his health.'

The furrowed brow cleared at once. 'I knew he suffered from some sort of chronic asthma, but I never realised it was quite so serious.'

'It's more serious than even I imagined,' she confessed.

Arthur Rennie's lined features softened as he studied Alison's slim, straight figure in the neat grey suit. 'I'll be sorry to lose you.'

'I've been very happy here, and I'll be sorry to leave, but . . .' she paused and gestured helplessly with her hands, 'I no longer have a choice. Ferdie's health is of prime importance at the moment.'

'Have you found another job up country?'

'Not yet, I——' She bit her lip nervously. 'I was hoping you wouldn't mind if I took off the rest of this week to go in search of something suitable.'

'I could hardly object in the circumstances.'

Alison sighed inwardly. She had not expected him

to be so accommodating, and relief brought a lump to her throat. 'You're very kind.'

'Think nothing of it,' her employer smiled thinly despite the irritation of knowing that he would soon lose one of his most efficient employees.

Alison still had to solve the problem of where to stay while she was in Stellenbosch. A hotel was quite out of the question. She needed to stay at a place where Ferdie could be taken care of while she was out most of the day seeking suitable employment, and the only person she could think of was Kate Duval. Kate *van der Bijl*, she corrected herself hastily. Alison had heard, via a mutual acquaintance, of the happenings out at the Solitaire estate. Kate's father had died almost two years ago, and a month after his death Kate had married Rhyno van der Bijl, her father's estate manager and winemaker. Alison had understood at the time that there had been a great deal of speculation concerning Kate's marriage to Rhyno. There had been a rumour that they had been forced into marriage in order to inherit Solitaire and the adjoining farm, La Reine, but, whatever the reason for their marriage, the gossips had apparently been proved wrong. Kate and Rhyno were, according to Alison's informant, happily married with a small daughter to bind their marriage even more securely.

Alison had been fond of Kate. They had both been twenty then, and Alison had looked forward to those frequent visits to Solitaire. She had found it bracing to be in Kate's vibrantly alive company, but that was four years ago, and Alison was not at all certain that Kate would welcome her in her home after all this time.

There was only one way to find out, Alison decided that evening after she had put Ferdie to bed and had made certain that he was asleep. She looked up Solitaire's number in the telephone directory, and she dialled it before she could lose her nerve. Several agonising seconds passed before a female, but a businesslike voice answered at the other end.

'Kate?' Alison queried, nervous anxiety making her uncertain as to the identity of the woman to whom she was speaking and, when she received a rather puzzled confirmation, she said hesitantly, 'It's Alison.'

'*Alison?*' Kate van der Bijl queried, and for a split second there was a stunned silence before she asked sharply and incredulously, '*Alison du Bois?*'

It had been a long time since anyone had called her Alison du Bois. After leaving Dirk all those years ago she had once more taken on her maiden name, Rousseau, and a strange shiver coursed its way along her spine at hearing herself addressed as Alison du Bois after all this time. She was still legally bound to Dirk, but it was a thought she seldom liked to dwell on, and it jarred her nerves to be reminded of it at that precise moment.

'Yes, that's correct,' she heard herself replying to Kate's query.

'Good heavens!' There was another brief silence while Kate seemed to absorb this startling information before she burst into excited speech. 'Where have you been all these years?'

Alison twisted the telephone cord nervously about her fingers. 'I've been living here in Cape Town.'

'But why didn't you write to me and let me know?'

'I wanted to at first, but then I thought it best not to.' Alison did not want to prolong the trend of this conversation on the telephone, and hastily came to the point. 'Kate, would you think me positively dreadful if I asked you to do me a favour?'

'If I can help you in any way, then you have only to say so,' Kate van der Bijl replied without hestitation, making Alison realise that she had not changed at all from the Kate she had once known.

'I need a place to stay for a few days.' She paused, took a deep breath, and added in a rush, 'For myself and my son.'

'Your *son*?' Kate exclaimed, and the line almost crackled with distinct curiosity.

'Look, I'll explain when I see you,' Alison promised hastily before Kate could fire a volley of questions at her. 'I have to find myself a job somewhere in Stellenbosch, or farther inland, and I need somewhere safe to leave Ferdie while I'm out job-hunting.' She paused for breath, hating herself for having to impose on Kate in this manner, but for Ferdie's sake she *had* to do it. 'Could you put us up for a few days?'

'I'll have a room prepared for you at once,' said Kate. 'When can we expect you?'

'We're leaving here early tomorrow morning.'

'Right.'

'And, Kate . . .' Alison gave the telephone cord an added twist around her fingers, 'can I depend on your silence?'

'If you mean will I keep my mouth shut if I should run into Dirk, then you have my word on that,' came the prompt and understanding reply.

'Thanks.'

Alison felt relieved when she replaced the receiver on its cradle, but she could not shake off that nervous feeling at the pit of her stomach. She took down a suitcase and packed her clothes and Ferdie's to keep herself occupied, but her mind would not be stilled. It could all have been so different if Dirk had made her feel, just *once*, that he had cared for her mind and her soul as well as her body. He had taken without giving in return, allowing her to come physically close to him, but always leaving her with the feeling that he had held back mentally something vital which could have led to a better understanding between them.

She pushed a thick strand of hair out of her eyes and tried to concentrate on her packing, but Dirk's harsh voice echoed from the shadowy chambers of her mind. 'If you walk out of this house now, then don't think I'll ever allow you to come back again.'

The pain was as raw as if he had spoken those words a minute ago. He had cared so little that he had issued her with an ultimatum instead of offering an explanation when, in the heat of the moment, she had threatened to leave him, and a future under his callous domination had been too frightening even to contemplate. She had packed her things, taking with her only the bare necessities, and had left Bordeaux without telling Dirk that she was going to have his child.

Alison could not imagine why she should be recalling the past so vividly after all this time. Perhaps her decision to return to the winelands had triggered off something which had opened up the sluice gates of her mind to let the painful memories flood her being so hauntingly, but whatever the cause it was near unbearable. She pressed her fingers against her throbbing temples and wondered if she was doing the right thing by wanting to make a home for Ferdie and herself in Stellenbosch. It was perhaps too close to the Paarl area where Dirk's estate was situated, but her mind had blanked out every other possibility. She loved this part of the country with its rugged mountains and deep valleys, and she could not bear the thought of moving farther north to another province. Living closer to Dirk's estate would have its disadvantages, but she was certain that she would be able to cope with whatever problems arose, and she could not foresee any reason why he should discover her presence in Stellenbosch.

After an uncommonly restless night Alison was up early the following morning to pack the last-minute things, and they left Cape Town shortly after breakfast. The traffic was heavy at that time of the morning, but once they left the city behind them she settled down and began to enjoy the countryside. Ferdie amused himself with a toy car for a while, but after half an hour he became restless.

'Where are we going, Mummy?' he asked for the third time that morning, and Alison sighed inwardly.

'I told you, we're going to Solitaire.'

'What's that?'

'Solitaire is a wine estate near Stellenbosch,' Alison explained patiently.

'What's a wine estate?'

'It's a farm where they grow grapes to make wine.'

'Oh.' He was silent for a moment as if he were digesting the information he had received, then he resumed his questioning. 'Why are we going to Sol— Sol——'

'Solitaire,' she helped him out tolerantly. 'We're going to stay with friends of mine.'

'For a holiday?' he asked eagerly, and she shook her head.

'We'll only be staying for a few days.'

'Is it still very far?'

'Not so very far,' Alison sighed, trying to concentrate on the road winding its way through the sun-drenched countryside. 'Why don't you lie down and take a nap for a while?'

'I'm not sleepy,' Ferdie argued stubbornly. 'I'm hungry.'

'There are biscuits in the tin at your feet,' she told him, and was glad that she had remembered at the last minute to bring along something to eat, since it kept Ferdie quiet and contented for the rest of the journey.

They drove through Stellenbosch with its oak-lined streets, and Alison admired the classic architecture of the buildings which had been preserved over the years. Alison did not pause to take in the details of her surroundings, but drove on through the town. Some fifteen minutes later she was entering the Solitaire estate through its majestic gates, and approaching the historic homestead with its Gothic gables etched proudly against the blue, cloudless sky.

She parked her Renault under a shady oak, and she and Ferdie had barely got out of the car when Kate van der Bijl emerged from the house and came walking

briskly towards them. Tall and slim, with her silvery
hair hanging loosely about her shoulders, she seemed
not to have changed at all in the four years since they
had last met, but as she came closer Alison noticed an
inner radiance and contentment in those sapphire
blue eyes which had not been there before.

'Alison!' Kate exclaimed as they embraced, smiled
at each other, and embraced again. 'Oh, it's good to
see you again!'

'It's been more than three years ... almost four,'
Alison conceded as they studied each other closely,
then Kate's glance shifted to the small boy who stood
observing them in silence with wide grey eyes.

'And this is?' Kate smiled enquiringly.

'Ferdie,' Alison introduced her son, her hand on his
shoulder propelling him a little forward. 'Say hello to
Aunty Kate.'

Very adult for his three and a half years, Ferdie held
out his hand politely, and Kate clasped it in her own.
They murmured the usual pleasantries to each other,
but Alison was not listening. She was studying Kate,
and she did not miss that strange light in her eyes
when she stared at Ferdie.

'I'll have one of the servants bring in your things,'
Kate announced at length, linking her arm through
Alison's and taking Ferdie's hand as she ushered them
into the house which Alison remembered so well.

They had tea in the spacious living-room with its
tall, old-fashioned windows, and its mixture of
modern and antique furnishings. Alison had always
loved this room, but on this particular occasion she
was too tense to admire its architectural beauty. The
heavy wooden beams against the ceiling had always
fascinated her, but she felt no enthusiasm for her
surroundings at that moment, and it was only when
Ferdie went out to play in the garden that she felt
herself relaxing a fraction.

'He's Dirk's child, isn't he.'

It was a statement, not a question, and Alison met Kate's steady blue gaze unwaveringly. 'Yes, he is.'

'Does Dirk know about him?'

'I never told him.'

'Alison . . .' Kate paused, seemingly at a loss for words, then she gestured expressively with her slender hands. '*Why?*'

It was an all-encompassing question, so typical of Kate, and Alison knew she owed it to Kate to explain why she had left the winelands all those years ago without a word to anyone.

'It simply didn't work out,' Alison told her briefly, still finding it difficult to speak of the incidents which had caused her so much pain.

'But you were so madly in love with him.'

'That was one of the problems.' Bitterness clouded Alison's eyes and curved her sensitive mouth. 'I loved *him*, but he didn't love *me*.'

Kate looked astounded. 'I always thought he was crazy about you.'

'He wanted me, Kate, but he never once said he loved me,' Alison voiced the source of her unhappiness. 'And then there was Yvette Paulson.'

'Ah, yes,' Kate murmured gravely. 'The daughter of one of the directors at the Stellenbosch Winery.'

'Exactly.'

On the low table between them an arrangement of late autumn roses filled the air with their balmy scent, and it was a poignant reminder to Alison of those few months she had lived at Bordeaux with Dirk.

'I know Yvette was always a regular visitor to Bordeaux, and she still is,' Kate inadvertently dropped a snippet of information about the happenings on Dirk's estate. 'But there was never anything between them, was there?'

'She was always ranking all over him, and he never rejected her,' Alison remarked disgustedly. 'Oh, Kate, things weren't going well for us, and Dirk and I had

had a flaming row the day before I went to the doctor to have my suspicions confirmed that I was pregnant. I did a lot of thinking that afternoon before I went home to give Dirk the news, and I'd come to the conclusion that I was equally to blame, but when I arrived at Bordeaux I found Dirk in his study with Yvette. As usual she was fawning all over him, and even when he saw me standing there watching them he made no attempt to push her away.'

'That was when you left?'

'After another terrific row, yes,' Alison nodded.

'Didn't he try to stop you?'

'No.' Alison winced inwardly at the memory. 'He said that if I left Bordeaux I wasn't to think I could ever come back again.'

'So you left without telling him you were going to have his child,' Kate supplemented with rare understanding.

'If I'd told him he would have insisted that I stay, and I wasn't prepared to continue with our marriage in those circumstances.'

'You said something on the telephone about hunting for a job,' Kate changed the subject, and Alison launched into yet another explanation.

'Ferdie suffers from asthma, and the doctor advised that I take him away from the coast. I thought at once of Stellenbosch here in the Eerste river valley, and I could remember how fresh and clean the air always smelled.' She smiled a little self-consciously. 'Dr Samuels says Ferdie should outgrow his ailment, and I couldn't think of any place healthier than here in the valley.'

Kate looked perturbed. 'What if Dirk finds out about Ferdie?'

'I doubt if we'll ever run into each other,' Alison brushed aside Kate's remark. 'Besides, I've been using my maiden name, Rousseau, and I shall go on using it.'

'When do you intend to start job hunting?'

'This afternoon.' Alison's grey-green glance mirrored uncertainty. 'Would you mind keeping an eye on Ferdie while I'm out?'

'Of course I shan't mind,' Kate assured her at once. 'He'll be company for Eloise.'

Alison met Eloise at the luncheon table. She was a chubby fifteen-month-old who captured Ferdie's avid attention where she sat on her high chair between Kate and Rhyno van der Bijl, and she possessed the unusual combination of her father's dark, bold eyes and her mother's silvery hair. Rhyno was not at all what Alison had expected. She had always imagined that the spirited and fiery Kate would marry someone whom she would dominate and overshadow completely, but Rhyno did not fit into that category at all. Tall, dark and lean, he had a stern, almost severe look about him which indicated that he was not the type to allow himself to be twisted around a woman's little finger, but there was also an underlying gentleness about him in the way he behaved towards Kate and Eloise. He adored them, that much was obvious, but his adoration could never be looked upon as a weakness. Alison liked him at once, and she sensed that the feeling was mutual, but she also sensed a fraction of disapproval in his manner towards her.

The latter became obvious when she arrived back at Solitaire the following afternoon after a fruitless day in town. Tea had been set out on the terrace on that warm afternoon, but only Rhyno was there helping himself to a cup of tea.

'I'm glad we have these few moments alone, Alison,' he frowned down at her when she joined him, and she decided despairingly that her best form of defence was to attack.

'You don't approve of me, do you, Rhyno?'

'I don't approve of what you did,' he stated bluntly and severely. 'Can you imagine how Dirk will react if he should find out after all this time that he has a three-year-old son?'

'I can imagine,' she acknowledged, shivering at the thought of the terrible fury she had witnessed only once during their brief marriage. 'Are you going to tell him?' she asked, holding her breath.

'That's your department,' Rhyno thrashed the ball into her court almost ruthlessly, 'but if I become a party to this deceit he's going to hate my guts afterwards.'

Alison had never thought of it that way, and guilt spiralled sharply through her. 'I shouldn't have come here, I can see that now.'

He put down his cup and there was gentleness in his touch when he gripped her shoulders. 'Alison, we love having you here, but you must tell Dirk about Ferdie.'

'It's too late,' she muttered, biting down hard on her quivering lip and blinking back the unexpected tears. 'It's three . . . almost four years too late.'

'It's never too late,' Rhyno argued quietly, but she shook her head unhappily.

'When I packed my bags and walked out almost four years ago, he made it quite clear that I could never come back.'

'He has the right to know he's fathered a child.'

'Why?' she demanded bitterly. 'So that he can take Ferdie away from me?'

'Dirk wouldn't do that,' Rhyno protested frowningly.

'Wouldn't he?' Her mouth curved cynically. 'How well do you know him?'

Rhyno turned towards the tray and poured himself another cup of tea while he spoke. 'I know him pretty well.'

'You obviously don't know him well enough. If you did you'd know he would take Ferdie away from me without so much as a flicker of concern for my feelings,' Alison remonstrated in a choked voice. 'He doesn't care about *me*, you see, but I know how much he would want his son.'

During the profound silence which followed Alison's exposé neither she nor Rhyno heard Kate step out on to the terrace, and after only a brief glance at Alison's tortured features she directed an accusing glance at her husband.

'Have you been upsetting Alison?' she demanded of him abruptly.

'I'm afraid so,' he sighed, a rueful smile curving his mouth as he surveyed the two women confronting him. 'But I meant well, and I can only hope Alison will believe that.'

'I do believe it,' Alison conceded at once with total honesty. 'I agree that Dirk ought to know about Ferdie, but I've left it much too late, and I'm inclined to feel that what he doesn't know now won't hurt him much, whereas *I'm* the one who'll be hurt once again if he should find out.'

Rhyno nodded, but it was not quite a nod of agreement, then he drained his tea-cup and excused himself.

'Any luck finding a job?' Kate asked when they were alone and she had poured their tea.

'None at all, I'm afraid,' Alison sighed, and grimaced. 'The vacancies that exist have such a meagre salary to go with them that I would only barely be able to support myself, let alone a child as well. I approached a few companies on the offchance that they might have something, and although the salary they could offer me would be good, the vacancies will only occur within a month or two, and I can't wait that long.'

'What are you going to do?' Kate asked worriedly.

'I think I'll have to forget about Stellenbosch and go farther north to Worcester,' Alison sighed once again, and there was a note of despair in her voice when she added: 'Who knows, I might find something there.'

A dusty jeep crunched up Solitaire's circular drive, but they took no notice of it, and it was only when it stopped beneath the shady oak that both Alison and Kate glanced in that direction.

'*Damn!*' Kate exclaimed angrily when that frighteningly familiar giant of a man emerged from the vehicle. 'I should have warned you that Dirk has a habit of dropping in unexpectedly from time to time to see Rhyno, and now I'm afraid it's too late to dash inside without being seen.'

Alison could not have moved even if she had wanted to. Her face had become as white as the plastered wall behind her chair, and a numbness had invaded her legs to keep her glued to her seat as she watched the tall, rugged-looking man striding towards them. Despite his size, Dirk's movements were as fluid and lithe as a jungle cat on the prowl, and she knew only too well the punishing strength of those large hands which he clenched briefly at his sides when at last they met face to face. His cold grey glance flicked over her with a lack of interest that stung for some unaccountable reason, and she gripped the arms of her chair tightly when she felt that sickening lurch of fear in her breast.

CHAPTER TWO

'How nice of you to pay us a visit, Dirk,' Kate broke
the frightening silence on the terrace in an attempt at
casualness, but Dirk gave her no more than a curt nod
before his icy glance slid back to settle on Alison.

'Hello, Alison,' he said evenly, the familiar deep
timbre of his voice vibrating across the ends of her
raw, quivering nerves. 'It's been a long time.'

'Yes,' she managed in no more than a croak, her
terrified eyes taking in the length and breadth of him
in khaki pants and bush jacket.

He had not changed much, she decided as she
studied him without actually being aware that she was
doing so. There was a premature sprinkling of grey
against his temples, and when she took a closer look
she realised that he had lost a considerable amount of
weight over the past years. He looked physically fit,
but there was a hollowness in his deeply tanned cheeks
which had not been there before, and the wide
shoulders seemed to taper down to much slimmer
hips.

'Could I offer you a cup of tea, Dirk?' Kate
attempted once again to break the awkward silence
which his dominant presence on the terrace had
created, and Alison quite suddenly came to her senses
with the realisation that Dirk had been studying her
with equal intensity.

'Not at the moment, thanks,' he declined Kate's
offer without taking his eyes off Alison, who sat
clutching the arms of her chair to hide the fact that her
hands were shaking. 'What are you doing here on
Solitaire, Alison?'

The shock of meeting him again made way for a

suffocating fear she could not control, and the only thought in her mind at that moment was that, somehow, she *had* to keep Ferdie out of his way.

'Alison is here as my guest for a few days while she has business to attend to in Stellenbosch,' Kate stepped into the breach, giving Alison time to gather her scattered wits about her.

'I think Alison is quite capable of speaking for herself,' Dirk remarked bitingly, and Kate was about to retaliate in a similar vein when Alison decided to intervene.

'It's all right, Kate,' she said hastily, her eyes darting a silent plea at her friend when the not too distant sound of a child's laughter reached their ears.

Kate understood the urgency of the situation, but before she could react, a small boy dressed in blue shorts and a sweater darted out on to the terrace.

'Mummy, Mummy, look what I've got!' Ferdie exclaimed excitedly, rushing towards Alison who had risen shakily from her chair with the futile desire to snatch up her child and run, but it was too late. Dirk's steely glance had darted in Ferdie's direction the moment he had appeared on the terrace, and the grim tightening of that strong mouth spoke volumes.

'Yes, darling, that's lovely,' Alison remarked, succeeding somehow to appear natural as she bent down to examine the yellow, fluffy chicken which Ferdie held so gently in his small hands. 'Now go and put it back where you found it.'

'Must I?' Ferdie demanded disappointedly.

'Yes, you must,' Alison insisted quietly, conscious of Dirk's glance flicking over them and taking in every detail of the child's features.

'Oh, all right,' Ferdie scowled, and then Kate was there, gently leading him away from the two people who stood facing each other in stony silence on the sunlit terrace.

Alison felt cold despite the warmth of the afternoon

sun, and the frightened thudding of her heart threatened to choke her when she found herself looking a long way up into Dirk's face which had gone strangely white about the mouth.

'*He's mine!*' his rasping voice finally broke the electrifying silence between them, and the fury in his eyes stabbed at her like heated swords. 'My God, you had my child, and all this time I never even knew!'

'What makes you think he's your child?' she demanded, fear and despair forcing her to try and bluff herself out of this dangerous situation, but she knew even then that it was futile.

'He's *mine!*' thundered Dirk, his large hands taking her shoulders in what felt like a crushing vice, and he shook her savagely until she was afraid that her neck would snap. 'Dammit, I'm not blind, so don't lie to me!'

'Take your hands off me,' she gasped when he finally gave her the opportunity to speak, but, instead of releasing her, he slid his hands to her throat and exerted a pressure with those strong-fingers that seemed intent upon obstructing her breathing.

'I could kill you for this,' he hissed through his teeth, and his features had become distorted in a savage mask that made her tremble with a fear so intense that she might have screamed if his fingers had not shut off her voice so effectively at the base of her throat.

'Dirk . . . please!' she finally begged chokingly, her hands clutching frantically at his strong wrists when she felt herself on the verge of sinking into a terrible darkness, and he released her at once with an exclamation on his lips which was a mixture of disgust and fury.

'Why didn't you tell me?' he demanded harshly while she stood swaying in front of him. 'Why did you go away and leave me in ignorance about the fact that I was to become a father?'

'Our marriage was over,' she managed somehow, clutching at a cane chair for support while she endeavoured to regain her breath as well as her composure. 'And I had no intention of staying with you simply for Ferdie's sake.'

'*Ferdie?*' he pounced on the name as he towered over her. 'You called him Ferdinand?'

She could still feel the frightening touch of his hands about her throat even though he had released her, and she swallowed nervously. 'I named him Dirk Ferdinand . . . after you.'

'I'm amazed to discover that in naming him you had the decency at least to acknowledge the fact that I'm his father,' he snarled at her, then he seemed to control himself, and that frighteningly cold mask settled back on his rugged face. 'Where have you been living all this time?'

'In Cape Town.'

'What are you doing here on Solitaire?' he demanded once again, his piercing glance holding hers captive. 'And this time I want the truth!'

'I'm looking for a job,' she confessed in a whisper, realising the futility of pretence, and the rest of it spilled out almost of its own volition. 'Ferdie suffers from asthma, and the doctor advised that I take him away from the coast.'

The knowledge of his son's ailment did not soften Dirk's features, and he barked out his next query. 'Did you find employment?'

'No.' Alison suppressed a sigh and the fire of the sun leapt in her dark hair as she lowered her head and let it fall forward to veil her expression of near defeat. 'Not yet.'

'I have a vacancy that needs filling on Bordeaux,' he announced after a lengthy, strained silence, and her head shot up, vague suspicion lurking in her grey-green eyes as they met his.

'What makes you think I have any desire to come back to you?'

'I don't recall asking you to come back to me,' he bit out the words, and a stinging warmth invaded her pale cheeks. 'I said I had a vacancy that needs filling. I need a P.R.O. out at the estate to cope with the public, and I need someone to act as hostess when I entertain my friends and business associates. My assistant has found himself a wife and they've moved into the house I had built for them. The flat in the old house has been standing vacant for some months now, and you could move in right away.'

Alison shrank from the thought of working for him and said stiffly, 'No, thank you.'

'I wouldn't decline my offer in such a hurry, if I were you,' he warned quietly in distinctly ominous tones.

'I'm returning to Cape Town in the morning, and I'll think of something else,' she argued, rejecting his suggestion with every part of her being.

'I'll give you a week to consider my offer.'

'I can give you my answer now, and it's the same as before.' She veiled the fear in her eyes and met the onslaught of his stabbing glance. 'No, thank you.'

'You'd be wise to think it over, Alison,' Dirk warned again, his mouth twisting savagely as he took a threatening pace towards her. 'Now that I know I have a son I mean to have him. Reject my offer without further thought and I might be tempted to take Ferdie with me now, and send you to hell!'

Alison's face went ashen as she stared up at him, and it felt to her as if she were seeing him for the first time. She had loved him once for his gentleness and concern, and she had loved him also for that unrelenting thread of steel woven into his character. She had never imagined he could be cruel, but now that cruelty was being savagely released, and she was at the receiving end of it.

'You would do that too, wouldn't you?' she

breathed huskily, her throat tight with frightened tears as she looked up into narrowed eyes that resembled slivers of ice.

'I never make idle threats.'

Anger was her only alternative to bursting into tears at the thought of losing Ferdie, and green fire sparked in her eyes as she hissed, 'You're a fiend!'

'Call me what you will, but I want my son with me on Bordeaux where he belongs,' his deep voice flicked raspingly across sensitive nerves as he delivered his ultimatum in further detail. 'I'm being more reasonable than you've been towards me. I've given you a choice, and I'm allowing you a week in which to consider it. You can have that job I offered you, which will mean that you can be with the boy, or you can refuse my offer and never see him again.'

Alison had always known that it would come to this if Dirk should ever find out about Ferdie, and she also knew that he meant every word he had said. He would take Ferdie away from her without one iota of concern for her feelings, and knowing that he was aware of how little she could do to prevent it sent a stab of pain through her.

'Ferdie is *mine*!' she argued in an anguished voice.

'He is also *my* son, and I will no longer be denied the right to him,' came the hatefully calm reply, then he thrust his diary and pen at her. 'Write down your address in Cape Town.'

'*No!*' she cried, recoiling from the thought of shutting off the only avenue of escape she still had left.

'*Write it down!*' Dirk thundered, standing over her while she found herself obeying him numbly and, when she had done as he had instructed, he took the diary from her and scrutinised what she had written down. 'This had better be the correct address, Alison. Before I leave here this afternoon I'm going to take down your car registration number as a safety measure, and I'll trace you through that if I find you've given me false information.' His hand gripped her wrist, his fingers biting into the soft flesh as he jerked her up against him so that she could see more clearly the ruthless twist of his mouth, and the cold fury in his narrowed eyes as they blazed down into hers. 'Try to escape me, my dear Alison, and you'll find yourself without the choice I've given you.'

His nearness brought memories surging back that did not bear thinking about at that moment. His masculine cologne mingled with the smell of the sun which clung to him, and the familiarity of it stabbed viciously at her senses until her limbs began to tremble beneath her with an inner weakness she despised.

'You're a swine, Dirk du Bois!' she fumed up at him, wrenching herself free of him, and of that diabolical magnetism which still had the power to affect the regular rhythm of her pulse.

'I shall expect to hear from you within the next week,' was all he said and, pocketing his diary and pen, he turned on his heel and strode away from her.

Alison did not wait to see whether he took down the registration number of her car, but, in her eagerness to get away, she rushed inside and almost collided with Kate in the spacious hall.

'What happened?' Kate demanded anxiously, her hands steadying Alison and ushering her into the living-room.

'Dirk has offered me a job as Public Relations Officer and hostess to his business associates on Bordeaux,' she almost spat out the words as Kate pushed her on to the sofa and sat down beside her. 'There's a flat in the old house which has gone vacant, and Ferdie and I could stay there.'

'Are you going to accept his offer?'

Bleak despair was mirrored in Alison's eyes. 'If I refuse then I lose Ferdie.'

'You mean he'll take him away from you?' Kate

questioned in near disbelief, and Alison nodded
slowly, sliding her hands beneath her hair and
combing it away from her white face with her fingers.

'He's given me a week to think it over.'

'That's *some* choice he's given you!' Kate exploded,
her sapphire blue eyes sparkling with anger.

'I don't know what I'm going to do,' Alison
groaned, the helplessness of someone condemned
settling about her until she could almost feel the
tightening of the noose about her neck.

'You can't let him take Ferdie away from you,' Kate
protested with a vehemence that was quite endearing.

'I can't let him take Ferdie away from me, and
neither can I bear the thought of returning to
Bordeaux.'

'You'll have to, I suppose, for the child's sake, and
your own,' Kate murmured fatalistically when she
began to see the total futility of Alison's predicament.

'Can you imagine what my life will be like if I
accept his offer?' The edge of bitterness was in
Alison's voice and in her eyes when they met Kate's.
'My life would be a living *hell*, but I also know it
would be a thousand times worse without Ferdie.'

'I wish I could help you.'

There was a certain amount of comfort in knowing
that Kate meant that sincerely, but it also brought
tears to Alison's eyes which she had to blink away
hastily as she rose to her feet. 'I'd better go and see
what Ferdie is up to before I pack our things. I want
to leave early in the morning.'

Life assumed almost nightmare proportions for Alison
during the week following her excursion out to
Stellenbosch. She had been given the choice to accept
what Dirk had to offer her, or to lose Ferdie
altogether, and the latter was totally unthinkable. She
was, actually, left with no choice at all, but her mind
continued its frantic search for an escape. It did not

make it any easier for her when Ferdie became ill towards the end of the week, and when nothing seemed to relieve the child's agonising struggle for breath Alison was forced to seek Dr Samuels' medical assistance.

Leonard Samuels arrived a few minutes after nine that evening and, after administering the necessary injection, he ushered Alison out of Ferdie's room with an angry frown creasing his brow.

'I don't want to sound as if I'm nagging you, Alison, but how soon can you get him away from this climate?'

She felt that proverbial noose tightening its pressure about her throat. 'I'd take him away tomorrow if I could, but I can't leave here for another week.'

'That's one week too long for that boy, and I *mean* it,' the doctor warned severely when she accompanied him to the door, and his concerned expression lingered when he paused to add: 'Don't hesitate to call me if there's no improvement within the next hour.'

Alison nodded mutely and tried to smile her thanks, but the tears were much too close, and her mouth quivered dangerously as she watched Dr Samuels walk towards the lift, then she closed the door and leaned against it dejectedly while she fought desperately to regain control of herself before she returned to Ferdie's side.

She sat beside his bed and held his hand while she attempted to return his steady, frightened glance with a calmness and assurance she was far from experiencing herself. It was sheer agony having to sit there watching him fight to draw air into his lungs, and once that was done he had to resume the effort to force the air out again. It tore at her heart to watch this fierce battle taking place in his small, frail body and, loving him as much as she did, she knew that, for the sake of Ferdie's health, she could no longer cling to him selfishly. Her own happiness was of no importance at all when it was weighed up against her son's health, and it was this realisation alone that helped her to come to terms with the unavoidable path she had to tread in the future.

Ferdie slipped into an exhausted sleep the moment his breathing became easier and, gently brushing a stray curl away from his damp forehead, she left his bedside to make the necessary telephone call which was to seal her fate.

'Du Bois,' a deep, abrupt voice barked into her ear moments later, and she lowered herself on to the upright chair beside the telephone when her legs began to shake uncontrollably beneath her.

'Dirk, I—it's Alison.'

There was a brief pause before he stated arrogantly, 'I gather you've decided to accept my offer.'

'You didn't give me much of a choice, did you?' she parried in defence, striving to keep her temper in check.

'You gave *me* no choice at all,' he reminded her in a voice that vibrated savagely across the line. 'You simply took from me the right to be there when my son was born, denied me the opportunity to see him grow, and left me in total ignorance. For that alone I feel I have the right to take him from you without the slightest twinge of conscience.'

'Would you take him now if I refused to work for you?' she questioned with that part of her mind which still refused stubbornly to accept the inevitable.

'Is there anything you can say in defence of yourself which would make me consider your feelings when you never once stopped to consider mine in this matter?' he counter-questioned.

Alison felt like an animal driven into a corner. 'I had my reasons for doing what I did.'

'Sure!' he barked abruptly, then he changed the subject. 'When can I expect you?'

'I have to work a further week's notice.' Her hand tightened on the receiver and a fine film of perspiration stood out on her forehead. This was the moment she dreaded most, but she had to go through with it. 'Dirk, I—I was wondering—about Ferdie——'

'What about him?' that deep voice demanded when she faltered in fear and anguish, and somehow she managed to scrape together the necessary courage to continue.

'I had to call the doctor in to him again this evening, and—and the situation has become somewhat urgent.'

'Do you have to stay on at your job for another week?'

'I can't leave them in the lurch.'

'Since when did you develop a conscience about such things?' Dirk demanded derisively, his well-aimed arrow finding its mark and rendering her momentarily speechless. 'If you want me to come and fetch him, then say so,' he instructed harshly.

'Would you?' she managed finally through dry, stiff lips. 'Would you fetch him as soon as possible and take him out to Bordeaux with you?'

Alison was amazed at herself. A month ago she would not have taken her son anywhere near the man who had fathered him, yet here she was almost begging Dirk to take Ferdie. What if he deliberately alienated the child from her during this period he would have Ferdie to himself?

'I'll be there at ten tomorrow morning,' Dirk's voice interrupted her irrational thoughts, but, instead of feeling relieved about the situation, she felt agitated and nervous. 'Was there anything else?'

'Yes!' she wanted to shout. 'Remember that Ferdie is *mine!*' She bit back the words, however, and decided wisely that this was not the moment for a display of possessiveness. 'No ... that was all,' she murmured feebly instead.

'I'll be there tomorrow at ten as I said,' Dirk announced, and ended their conversation with an abrupt, 'Goodnight.'

Alison replaced the receiver and sat for a moment with her head dejectedly in her hands. She tried to tell herself that she had done the right thing, but a part of her remained wary and filled with the gravest doubts. She felt too tired at that moment to ponder the wiseness of her decision and, getting to her feet, she walked slowly out of the lounge and into Ferdie's room. The night had only just begun for her and, seated in an armchair beside his bed, she maintained an exhausting vigil through the hours until dawn. She dropped off to sleep a few times, but she was awake the moment Ferdie stirred to check his pulse and respiration.

There was no time to catch up on lost sleep the following morning. She had to telephone her employer to let him know she would be coming in to the office late, and after breakfast she packed a suitcase for Ferdie.

'Where are we going?' he wanted to know, his features revealing all the signs of his recent ordeal as he eyed the suitcase on his bed while Alison helped him into shorts and a shirt.

'*I'm* not going anywhere, darling, but *you* are,' she told him, sitting back on her heels to neaten the collar of his shirt and to fasten the buttons of his cardigan.

'Where am I going?'

Alison hesitated momentarily. Ferdie had asked her only once before about his father, and she had answered vaguely that his father had chosen not to live with them. He had accepted her explanation without comment at the time, but she wondered now how he was going to accept what she had to tell him.

'Your daddy is coming to fetch you,' she told him, observing him closely, and a stubborn expression flitted across his pale, thin face.

'I don't have a daddy.'

'Yes, you have,' she insisted gently but firmly, and took his face between her hands, forcing him to look at her. 'Do you remember that man who came to Aunty Kate's house while we were there?'

'I think so,' he frowned. 'Was that my daddy?'

'Yes.'

His lips quivered suddenly, and the wide grey eyes filled with tears. 'Why am I going with him? Why can't I stay here with you?'

'Ferdie, listen to me, darling.' She pulled him down on to her lap and stroked his hair tenderly when he pressed his face into her shoulder. 'You haven't been well lately, and Dr Samuels says you'll be much better if you go away from Cape Town.'

'Then you're coming too?' he asked, raising his head to look at her expectantly, and she hastily swallowed down the lump in her throat.

'Yes, darling, but I can't leave yet because I still have to go to work for another week before I can leave here,' she explained carefully. 'In the meantime it will be best for you to go and stay with your daddy on his estate until I can join you there.'

Ferdie was normally very adult for his age, but at that precise moment he was a very unhappy three-year-old at the thought of parting from his mother. 'I don't want to go without you.'

To have explained to him how much it hurt her to let him go without her would not have made it any easier for him, so she forced a smile to her unwilling lips, and made light of the subject. 'It will only be for eight days, then we'll be together again.'

Ferdie considered this for a moment, then he demanded childishly, 'Promise?'

'I promise,' Alison answered sincerely, then she hid her tears behind a laugh as she hugged him tightly and rocked him gently in her arms.

'Why has my daddy never stayed with us?' Ferdie wanted to know when she finally released him to pack the last few items of clothing he would require.

Alison did not quite know how to answer that

question. Ferdie was too young to understand the emotional turmoil and all the heartache which had led up to her decision to walk out on her husband and her marriage. He would not understand a woman's need to know that she was loved and not simply desired, and how could she explain her feeling of insecurity when Dirk had seemed so intent upon breaking down her trust in him instead of attempting to build it up?

'It's a long and involved story, Ferdie,' she sighed eventually, a sad smile curving her mouth as she stretched out her hand and pushed her fingers playfully through his dark curls. 'Perhaps I'll tell you some day.'

It was almost time for Dirk to arrive before Alison had an opportunity to do something about her own appearance. The face that stared back at her in the mirror looked pale, and lack of sleep had left a bruised look about her eyes which she was unable to disguise entirely, but with the aid of make-up she at least succeeded in putting a little colour into her cheeks. She brushed her hair and tied it into a casual knot in the nape of her neck, but there was no time to do more before the doorbell chimed.

Ferdie stood in the centre of the lounge, small and statue-like except for the anxiety in his eyes as he followed Alison's progress across the room. He looked as nervous and tense as she felt, and she hid the sudden tremor in her hands by unnecessarily straightening the folds of her skirt. Outwardly calm and composed at last, she glanced over her shoulder to smile encouragingly at Ferdie, then she took a steadying breath and opened the door.

Dirk filled her doorway, and he looked so vitally male in brown corded pants and jacket that Alison was reminded of the first time they had met. She had felt threatened then, and she felt equally threatened now as his cold grey glance slid over her, but on this occasion it was for a totally different reason. She was about to place in his hands the most lethal weapon he could wish for if he should wish to destroy her, but she had to take that chance for Ferdie's sake.

'Please come in,' she heard herself say in a voice that sounded surprisingly cool, and she felt certain that not even he could guess at the shattering effect his presence had on her.

'So this is where you've been hiding away all these years,' he remarked derisively as he stepped inside, but she chose to ignore that verbal stab as she shut the door against the south-easterly breeze which had sprung up early that morning. Dirk's sweeping glance skipped over the simple furnishings and finally settled on the small boy who stood observing him so intently from the opposite side of the room. For seemingly endless seconds neither of them spoke, and Alison found herself mentally holding her breath. It was as if they were determinedly summing each other up, then a faint smile curved Dirk's chiselled mouth as he went forward and held out his hand in a formal gesture of greeting. 'Hello, Ferdie.'

Ferdie darted an uncertain glance in Alison's direction, but when she nodded encouragingly he placed his small hand in Dirk's with a husky, 'Hello.'

'Has your mother told you who I am?' Dirk questioned him.

Ferdie nodded, darting another quick glance at Alison who stood observing them in silence. 'She said you're my daddy.'

'Come here,' said Dirk, drawing him towards the sofa so that they could sit down beside each other and, watching them, Alison experienced a strange stirring deep within her. 'Will you come and stay with me for these few days so that we can get to know each other?' Dirk was asking Ferdie.

The child's grey eyes sought Alison's as if to remind her silently of the promise he had extracted from her earlier that morning, and she nodded unobtrusively, but Dirk's keen glance had intercepted that silent communication between mother and son.

'You could help me clean up the place a bit so that it looks nice when your mother comes,' Dirk suggested with an understanding Alison had not expected of him, and she saw the uncertainty drain slowly from Ferdie's pale face.

'Okay, I'll come,' Ferdie smiled shyly.

'Good!' Dirk's manner was abrupt as usual, but the large hand that brushed over Ferdie's hair was gentle, and there was a strangely distant look in those steel-grey eyes while he sat observing his son.

'Could I make you a cup of coffee?' Alison offered in an attempt to delay the parting, but Dirk dashed her hopes by declining.

'I have to get straight back,' he said, getting to his feet as if to underline the fact. 'Is there anything I ought to know? Such as what medication to use if it should become necessary?'

'You'll find everything you may need in here.' She picked up a small vanity case and held it out to him. 'The use of each medication is clearly marked.'

'Are we going now?' Ferdie wanted to know when Dirk picked up the suitcase which Alison had placed beside the sofa some minutes before Dirk's arrival.

'There's no sense in wasting valuable time,' Dirk announced, and all Alison's feelings seemed to have centred themselves in a hard lump at the base of her throat when she took Ferdie's hand in her own and followed Dirk from the flat.

In the confined space of the lift Alison observed Dirk covertly. It was difficult to believe that she was actually still married to this harsh-faced man who was so familiar to her in some ways, yet so much a stranger in others, and it was even more difficult to believe that, for a few brief months, she had lived with him as his wife. She had never been allowed to delve into the essence of this man she had once loved, and the thoughts behind those steel-grey eyes still remained as much a mystery to her now as then. It was as if he had taken pains to close the door to his soul, forbidding her to enter, and the knowledge that she was being shut out was one of the many reasons why she had left him all those years ago.

Between them, his head tilted at a proud angle like his father's, stood the product of those brief months. For almost three and a half years Alison had hidden his existence from Dirk, but now fate was forcing her to deliver Ferdie into his father's hands, and something warned her that this was only the first of many sacrifices she would have to make in future.

A sleek white Jaguar was parked in the quiet street outside the building. Dirk deposited Ferdie's suitcase in the boot, and there was a hint of displeasure in his glance when he turned to see Ferdie still clinging tightly to Alison's hand.

'Say goodbye to your mother,' he said authoritatively.

Goodbye! Dirk made it sound so terribly final, Alison thought as she lifted Ferdie into her arms to hold his small body close against her, and she had difficulty in blinking back the tears when she felt his arms tightening about her neck.

'Don't forget,' Ferdie said close to her ear, but he spoke loud enough for Dirk to hear. 'You promised.'

'I shan't forget,' Alison replied, not daring to glance in Dirk's direction when he stepped past them to open the car door for her to place Ferdie on the front seat.

She adjusted the seat-belt and fastened it about his small body and, when she finally stepped back to let Dirk close the door, she found herself marvelling at how swiftly a child could adapt to circumstances. While *she* was still choked with unshed tears at the thought of parting from him, Ferdie was totally fascinated by the knobs and dials on the Jaguar's intricate dashboard, and for a moment she could not make up her mind whether to laugh or cry.

'What promise did you have to make the boy?' Dirk demanded behind her, and she controlled her features swiftly before she turned to face him.

'I had to promise him we would be together again in eight days' time before he would agree to go with you.'

Contempt, bitingly cold, was in the eyes that flicked over her. 'You made a promise to me once, and you never considered that as binding.'

The accusation stung, the truth biting into her soul as an arrow would bite into exposed flesh, and her only defence against the pain was an anger which made her normally soft, husky voice sound as brittle as ice.

'Do we have to rake up the past?'

'The past is an integral part of the present and the future, just as Ferdie is a part of you and me,' he reminded her harshly. 'You can't deny the past, just as you can't deny Ferdie's existence, so I suggest you accept it instead of trying to ignore it.'

He swung away from her, his long legs taking him round the bonnet of the car before she had time to think up a suitable reply. Moments later he was speeding away from her, and he took with him the only living person who belonged to her, and to whom she had truly belonged.

CHAPTER THREE

DARK clouds gathered in the sky on the day Ferdie left for Bordeaux with his father and, helped on by near gale force winds, the storm raged violently across the peninsula for the duration of the weekend before easing off until the rain was no more than a fine spray. Alison found it almost unbearable in the flat without Ferdie, and the weather seemed to express exactly how she felt inside; cold and miserable. She was grateful, all the same, that Ferdie had escaped the dampness which prevailed in the air at the coast. Everything she touched felt clammy, even her clothes, and common sense finally assured her that she had done the right thing to send her son away, even though she still nurtured certain doubts about the wiseness of letting him stay with Dirk for these eight days.

'I always maintained that it was wrong of you not to let your husband know he had a son,' Dr Samuels announced when she telephoned him to tell him about Ferdie, and his remark added weight to that feeling of guilt she had laboured under during the past years. 'Your decision to let him take Ferdie out to his estate will not only enhance the child's chances of overcoming his problem, but it will give them the opportunity to get to know each other, and that's as it should be. A boy, especially, needs his father as well as his mother.'

Wise words, Alison had thought afterwards, and they had made sense too. But how could she explain the fears that lurked in the recesses of her mind? If Dirk was contemplating revenge, then it would be the easiest thing on earth for him to turn her away when she arrived at Bordeaux, and because she had been the

42

one to walk out on him in the first place, he would quite rightly have the law on his side if he claimed custody of Ferdie.

She shivered at the thought and tried to thrust it from her, but it plagued her mercilessly for the next few days. A part of her doubted very strongly that Dirk would ever do such a thing, but then there was also a part of her that was not so sure. Dirk could be cruel, if he wished, and what better way to take his revenge for what she had done to him?

Alison's spirits were at their lowest ebb the Tuesday morning when Kate telephoned her at the office with the invitation to join her for lunch in town, and she accepted Kate's invitation without hesitation. Seeing Kate again would be like a breath of fresh air in this dismal world she had plunged into, and there was just the slightest possibility that Kate might have some news of Ferdie. Later, when she was on her way to meet Kate, it occurred to her that she had never informed Kate of the latest developments, and it was not without a certain amount of guilt that Alison faced her friend across the small table in the beachfront restaurant of Kate's choice.

Slim, fair, and elegant in a wine-red woollen dress with a gold chain dangling about her slender throat, Kate made Alison feel vaguely envious while they sat waiting for their crayfish lunch to be served. Alison was suddenly very aware of her unattractive grey, tailored suit with the crisp white blouse which she had always found suitable for the office. It was neat and inexpensive, but not at all stylish in comparison with Kate's outfit, and Alison was forced to recall that Kate had never had to think twice about spending money for fear of it not lasting until the end of each month. It was a known fact that Kate came from a wealthy family, but she had never been blasé about it, and Alison had always admired her for that.

She sighed inwardly now as she recalled her own

struggle to make ends meet over the past years, but it had given her a sense of achievement in the end to know that she had succeeded without having to ask for help from anyone.

'I believe Ferdie is staying with Dirk at Bordeaux,' Kate finally touched on the subject which lay closest to Alison's heart.

'Yes, that's correct,' Alison confirmed while she made an attempt to eat her salad. 'I had to let him go on ahead of me when the doctor insisted that Ferdie should get away from here as soon as possible.'

'You've accepted Dirk's offer?'

'You know as well as I do that I had no choice,' Alison sighed, meeting Kate's steady, perturbed glance. 'I'll be going to Bordeaux this coming Saturday.'

Alison mentally crossed her fingers when she added the latter, and they finished their meal in silence.

'I don't mean to pry, Alison,' Kate resumed their conversation when their coffee had been placed in front of them, 'but how do you feel about Dirk?'

'If you mean do I still love him, then the answer is "no",' Alison replied with a quiet vehemence that surprised even herself. 'My feelings for him died a long time ago.'

Kate's expression gave away none of her thoughts, but then Alison remembered how adept Kate had always been at hiding her feelings when she wished.

'If you ever need any help, or perhaps someone simply to talk to, then don't hesitate to call me,' Kate offered, and Alison's heart warmed with affection towards her.

'You're being extraordinarily kind, Kate.'

'I've lived through some bad times myself,' Kate confessed with a faintly haunted look leaping into her eyes as if the memory of those 'bad' times still had the power to hurt her. 'I had my Aunt Edwina in whom I could confide, and from whom I could seek advice, but you have no one, and I would consider it an honour if you would trust me enough to make use of me.'

'Thank you, Kate,' Alison smiled, blinking back the tears which seemed to come so easily lately, then she changed the subject. 'Is your aunt still alive?'

'Very much so,' Kate laughed softly, pushing her empty cup aside and dabbing lightly at the corners of her mouth with her table napkin. 'Aunt Edwina spends most of the year travelling about, visiting friends and touring the country, but she always returns to Solitaire for Christmas and stays on through the harvest when every extra pair of hands on the estate comes in useful.'

Alison's grey-green eyes clouded. 'I hope my visit to your home hasn't caused unnecessary ill-feeling between Dirk and Rhyno?'

'None at all,' Kate assured her at once. 'As a matter of fact we've been invited to dinner at Bordeaux this evening.'

They chatted a little while longer before Alison glanced frowningly at her wrist watch. 'I must get back to the office.'

'And I must get back to Solitaire,' Kate confessed, glancing at her own watch as they pushed back their chairs and rose to their feet.

Kate settled the bill, refusing to accept Alison's offer to pay her share, and when they stepped out into the street Kate placed her hand lightly on Alison's arm.

'I'm so glad you could meet me for lunch, and I hope we're going to see more of you in future,' she smiled, and when she walked towards her white Mercedes Alison found herself echoing the wish that she would have the opportunity to resume her friendship with Kate van der Bijl.

The rest of the day passed slowly, but not unbearably so, although the following evening Alison found that she could no longer suppress the desire to telephone Bordeaux for news of her son and, after making herself something to eat, she dialled the estate's number.

'How is Ferdie?' she asked without preamble when she heard Dirk's deep voice on the telephone.

'He's well, but I don't think I should let you speak to him. I don't want him unsettled.'

The finality in his voice frightened her, but she was determined not to give way to her fears. 'Will you tell him I called?'

'I'll tell him.' A strained silence followed, then Dirk asked abruptly, 'Any messages?'

Her fear eased a little. 'Just tell him I love him, and that I'm counting the days until we're together again.'

'I hope you're not imagining that your stay here at Bordeaux is going to be a holiday for you?'

'You offered me a job, and I intend to execute it to the best of my ability,' Alison retorted in anger, but she could not deny to herself that she was also vaguely pleased. His remark did not indicate that he would do any of the things she had feared, and she found herself thinking that perhaps she had been quite wrong when she had imagined that Dirk would seek revenge.

'When can we expect you?' he allayed her fears to an even greater extent.

'I'll be leaving here early Saturday morning.'

'The flat should be ready for you when you arrive,' he informed her, and after thanking him politely she ended the conversation.

Alison's hands were shaking and her mouth felt dry when she had replaced the receiver on its cradle. She felt disturbed, yet somehow elated, but it had nothing to do with the sound of that deep voice which still seemed to ring in her ears. *Nothing* at all, she told herself convincingly. She had meant every word when she had told Kate that she no longer loved Dirk, and if his voice somehow still had the power to disturb her, then it was purely a physical reaction to something which she had once found pleasant.

Alison took a book to bed with her that evening and read until late, but when she eventually put out the light she found she could not sleep. Her mind was whirling in endless circles, taking her back in time. Too far back for comfort, she decided grimly as she tossed restlessly between the sheets in an effort to shut out the images that flashed before her eyes like haunting pictures from the past which she had thought she had buried.

'You're lovely, so very lovely,' Dirk's deep, vibrant voice was murmuring, and she saw again his grey eyes darkening with desire as they had acquainted themselves with every curve of her body.

The terror of her wedding night was upon her, and it was so real that her breathing quickened until the perspiration stood out on her forehead like tiny pearls on her pale skin. She had been afraid of that terrible passion which she knew Dirk had kept so tightly leashed before their marriage, but she had been even more afraid of the passion he had aroused in her. He had been gentle with her at first, she could not deny that, and he had aroused her to a peak where she had cast aside her painful shyness. He had undressed her in between sensual caresses, and it was then that he had devoured her untutored body with his eyes while he had murmured thickly, 'You're lovely, so very lovely, Alison.' What happened afterwards was still like a nightmare. His desire, unleashed, had been quite savage, and he had not spared her until he had awakened feelings in her which had been so primitive that she had wept silent tears of shame and fear long after he had fallen asleep beside her.

Alison sat up in bed, her breath coming in little sobs, and she was perspiring freely despite the coolness of the night. This side of her marriage to Dirk was something she seldom allowed herself to think about, but now these thoughts could not be held back. *Why?* she asked herself. Why *now?* She groaned and buried her face in her hands, but the memory would not be shut out, and the images flashed mercilessly through her mind.

She had perhaps been too young, and too inexperienced when she had married Dirk. The fierce flame of his desire for her had kindled a similar fire in her, and she had been too innocent at the time to cope. She had been a virgin in mind and body, and the pagan emotions he had awakened in her had frightened her beyond reason, but yet she had been drawn to him relentlessly like a moth to a flame.

'Oh, God!' she groaned, falling back weakly against the pillows. 'Please don't let me love him again. Please don't let me fall into that same trap.'

Alison finally drifted into an uneasy sleep, but she was never quite free of these disturbing thoughts during the following day while she tried to concentrate on her work, and neither was she free of them that evening when she sorted out her personal things from those which belonged to the furnished flat she had rented.

When her telephone rang shortly after eight her first thought was that Ferdie must be ill, but when she snatched up the receiver it was Kate's voice that came over the line.

'I thought I'd let you know,' she said. 'We saw Ferdie the other evening, and he's looking well.'

'Is he happy to be with Dirk?'

'He appears to be quite happy,' Kate assured her. 'He follows Dirk about like a shadow, and Dirk seems to enjoy taking Ferdie along with him wherever he goes.'

'I—I'm glad,' murmured Alison, trying to smother that faint twinge of unreasonable jealousy which shot through her.

'I was allowed to have a peep at the flat you'll be

moving into,' Kate went on. 'It's very nicely furnished, and Ferdie was telling me all about how he helped Salome wash down all the walls and clean out the cupboards.'

Alison's interest quickened. 'Is Salome still at Bordeaux?'

'I doubt if she'll ever leave,' Kate laughed softly. 'Her family have lived there for generations, and she neither knows nor wants any other kind of life.'

'It makes me happy to know that there'll be at least one familiar face on the estate.'

'There'll be plenty of familiar faces,' Kate told her. 'Do you remember Mike Petzer, Dirk's assistant? Mike is married now, but he's still there on Bordeaux. The office staff have changed over the years, but the household staff are still the same, and they told me they were looking forward to your return.'

Alison did not reply to this, but when they had ended their conversation she found herself hoping that Dirk's faithful Coloured workers would not be disappointed when they discovered that she would not be stepping back into her former place as his wife. That was something she would *never* do.

Alison felt simultaneously exhausted and elated when she handed in the keys to her flat the Saturday morning and slid behind the wheel of her loaded Renault. After putting in a full day at the office she had spent almost the entire evening packing her things, but now, at last, she was on her way to Bordeaux and Ferdie, and what she could not take with her in the car she had arranged to have sent on by rail.

She turned the key in the ignition and eased her foot off the clutch, but her mind was not on what she was doing. She knew what she was leaving behind, but she had no idea what she was going to, and all that she had to console herself with was the knowledge that she would be reunited with her small son. She put her foot down on the accelerator, in a hurry now to reach her destination, and as she turned on to the road that led to Paarl she caught a final gimpse of Table Mountain shrouded in those familiar mist clouds on that bleak June morning.

It was not much more than an hour's drive to Paarl with its distinctive landmark consisting of those three enormous granite boulders on the mountain which at times resembled pearls. Paarl, Britannia, and Gordon's Rock they had been named, and when Alison finally caught sight of them she felt a strange tension coiling up within her. This was where she had met Dirk for the first time, but she did not want to think of the past now. She had to concentrate on her driving and on the future.

Bordeaux lay to the south-east of Paarl, between the Paarl and Klein Drakenstein mountains, and when she turned off towards the estate on the outskirts of the town her hands tightened almost spasmodically on the steering wheel. Within less than ten minutes she was approaching the impressively arched stone entrance to Bordeaux. Beyond it lay the vineyards, the vines bereft of leaves except for a crimson few which still clung stubbornly, and a suffocating tightness seemed to grip her lungs as she drove up the familiar tree-lined avenue towards the gabled buildings.

The old homestead had not been in use for more than twenty years except as offices for the staff and storage space, and it also contained the flat which Alison would occupy during her stay on the estate. It was, however, towards the new gabled homestead that she steered her biscuit-coloured Renault. For practical reasons Dirk's late father had built this sturdy house for his family, but he had taken great care to maintain the old Cape Dutch style which was so familiar in the winelands.

Old oaks with gnarled stems cast a welcome shade in which to shelter from the blazing sun which sparkled on the old-fashioned windows of the house, and when she had parked her car in the shade her glance went involuntarily towards the large, ornately carved door with its heavy, and highly polished brass knocker which gleamed in the morning sunlight. Alison was seeing everything through a haze of something close to pain. There was a tightness in her chest which restricted her breathing, and when she got out of her car it felt to her as if she were stepping back into the past. She had once thought of this house as her home, and she had spent many tranquil hours in the garden with its smooth lawn bordered by colourful flowers and shrubs. It had all been so long ago, but now it felt to her as if time had stood still. The four years seemed to shrink until it felt as if she had been away no more than a day, and the feelings that surged through her at that moment were almost frightening.

'Mummy, Mummy!'

Alison surfaced sharply from her turbulent thoughts to see a small tornado emerging from the house to come racing towards her across the lawn. Everything else was forgotten and thrust aside firmly in that moment as she opened her arms to receive her child, and when she held him pressed against her she could not prevent the tears that filled her eyes and spilled from her lashes.

'Oh, Ferdie, I missed you!' Her voice was a choked whisper as she knelt on the grass and held him a little away from her to look into his happy, smiling face which was beginning to lose that familiar pale and pinched look. 'And you're looking so well,' she added, smiling through her tears.

'I haven't been sick once,' he confided with pride and delight at what he obviously considered a personal achievement, and he wound his arms tightly about her neck when she hugged him close once more.

Over Ferdie's dark head she saw Dirk observing them from a short distance away, and there was an unfathomable expression in his narrowed eyes that made her feel uneasy. His thumbs were hooked into the belt hugging his khaki pants to his lean hips, and the white shirt strained in a familiar manner across the wide expanse of his chest, but it was his ruggedly handsome features that caught and held her attention a fraction longer. Had she imagined it, or had she seen an amused, vaguely tender smile lurking about that strongly chiselled mouth?

'Welcome to Bordeaux,' said Dirk, and she was aware suddenly that her heart was beating fast against her ribs as she disentangled herself from Ferdie and rose to her feet.

'Am I really welcome?' she asked, unobtrusively dashing away the dampness of tears on her cheeks.

'I always do my best to make all my employees feel at home.'

His cutting reply was like a slap in the face. She had not intended her query to sound personal, but Dirk had obviously interpreted it in that manner, and a wry smile curved her soft mouth when she realised that she had been put firmly in her place. She was to be his employee, nothing more, and that, she told herself, was how she would prefer it.

'Come on, Mummy,' Ferdie urged, tugging at her hand. 'Let me show you where we're going to stay.'

Dirk fell into step beside them, shortening his long strides to accommodate Alison and Ferdie as they walked the short distance towards the old homestead. Ferdie babbled all the way, and it eased the strained silence which had settled between Dirk and Alison.

The flat was as she had remembered it when Mike Petzer had still lived there. The rooms were spacious, and the high ceilings had those heavy, old-fashioned wooden beams running across them. A few alterations had been made to modernise the flat, such as built-in cupboards in the bedrooms, and an additional bathroom which led off the main bedroom. It was comfortable and roomy, with two bedrooms, a lounge, dining-room, and a kitchen, and it was sparsely but adequately furnished with an odd assortment of old and new furniture, some of which she recognised as having belonged in the main house.

Ferdie literally dragged Alison excitedly from room to room, explaining in detail as they went how he and Salome had washed the walls and had scrubbed the floors before giving them a coat of wax until the yellow-wood surface gleamed richly once again.

'Do you like it?' Ferdie wanted to know in an oddly anxious manner when they returned to the lounge where Dirk stood leaning against the stinkwood writing desk.

'It's very nice,' she replied guardedly, aware of Dirk observing her with hooded eyes.

Her reply seemed to satisfy Ferdie, and his eyes were alight with eager excitement as he darted across the room and flung himself into the big, padded armchair in front of the large stone fireplace.

'Daddy says that when it's very cold we can have a fire and sit here in front of it to keep warm.'

Daddy! He had called Dirk *Daddy*, and it had tripped as easily off Ferdie's lips as it had startled her to hear him address Dirk in that manner.

'That will be lovely,' she heard herself saying as she glanced covertly at Dirk, and she glimpsed something close to a challenge in his eyes as if he dared her to deny that he had as much right to Ferdie as she had.

'If you'll give me the keys to your car, then I'll arrange for it to be brought up here,' Dirk instructed when she turned from his disturbing and challenging stare, and when she placed the small bunch of keys in his large hand, he added brusquely, 'I'll give you the rest of the day to settle in, but I want to see you in my study at five-thirty sharp this evening.'

He did not wait for her to reply, but strode out of the door and left her alone with Ferdie to explore the flat once more without his disturbing presence.

On this second tour of the flat Alison discovered that Ferdie's clothes had all been neatly packed into the cupboard in the bedroom opposite her own, and when they finally returned to the lounge she was surprised to discover that someone had carried in all the suitcases and boxes which she had brought with her in the car. She extended her exploration into the kitchen before unpacking, and she was pleasantly relieved to find that the cupboards as well as the refrigerator had been stocked to the hilt with everything and anything she could possibly require.

'Daddy sent Salome into town yesterday to do the shopping for you,' Ferdie answered her unspoken query, and then, almost as if the mention of her name had been a cue, Salome entered the kitchen through the back door which had stood slightly ajar.

'Good morning, madam.'

'Salome!' Alison exclaimed, pleasure lighting up her features as she stared into the smiling face of the big, buxom woman in the neat pink overall with the inevitable scarf of a matching colour tied about her head. 'Oh, Salome, it's good to see you again!'

Salome took the hand Alison extended towards her and bobbed a slight curtsey of respect. 'I am also very happy that the madam has come back to Bordeaux, but it troubles me that you are going to live here instead of in the big house with Master Dirk.'

Alison's expression sobered. 'I've come back here to work, Salome, and because I'm hoping that the climate here in the valley will be good for my son.'

The Coloured woman's glance rested momentarily on Ferdie before returning to Alison, and there was confusion in those dark eyes as she shook her head without probing further. Alison was Dirk's wife, and Ferdie was their son. To Salome that meant that they belonged together as a family under the same roof, and Alison could almost sense that Salome was thinking she would never quite understand the sometimes peculiar behaviour of the white people.

'Can I make you some tea, madam?'

At the mention of tea Alison realised how parched her throat felt, and Dirk's welcome had not extended to any form of refreshment.

'That would be lovely, Salome, but——' Uncertainty made her pause momentarily, and her wary glance sought Salome's. 'Wouldn't I be taking you away from your work?'

'*This* is my work, madam,' Salome informed her with a beaming smile. 'From today I cook for you, clean house for you, and look after Ferdie. Master Dirk's orders.'

Salome's words still echoed in Alison's ears when she returned to the lounge moments later. *Master Dirk's orders*. It was final, absolute, and not to be questioned. When Dirk gave an order it was carried out at once, and no one dared to argue. He was the master, his word was law, and Alison, heaven help her, was still one of his subjects.

Salome carried in a tray of tea and biscuits, creating a welcome diversion from the troubled thoughts racing through Alison's mind. Ferdie settled himself on a chair with a handful of biscuits, and Alison did not need to press him for information of his stay on Bordeaux without her. He had grown fond of Dirk, that much was obvious to her, but she was not quite certain whether she ought to feel pleased about it, or wary of the bond which was being forged so strongly between father and son.

Restless, and with an energy which was new to Alison, Ferdie went outside to play while Alison and Salome started to unpack. The hours passed with an incredible speed and, although they had paused for lunch, Alison could barely recall what she had eaten, and it was four o'clock before the flat was tidy and all the empty boxes and suitcases had been stowed away.

Tired and desperately in need of a bath, Alison left Salome to see to the last few things while she walked quickly down the short passage to her room. In the adjoining bathroom she ran her bath water and stripped down to her skin before she pushed her shoulder-length hair into a shower cap. She sprinkled a liberal amount of effervescent salts into the water, and finally stepped into it to soak for a few minutes until the tiredness drained out of her body.

It was a strange feeling to know that she was on Bordeaux soil once again. She had left almost four years ago with the intention of never returning, but at that time she had not imagined that the child she was carrying would one day force her into a situation where she would have to be at Dirk's mercy again. She sighed heavily as she felt herself relaxing in the bath with that familiar silence all around her. She had forgotten how silent it could become on the estate at this time of the day with nothing but the sounds of nature to disturb the peace, but it was a silence that soothed rather than depressed.

Alison dressed with more care than usual when she finally emerged from the bathroom. She selected a long-sleeved dress with a modest neckline, the vivid splashes of blue and green a perfect foil for her creamy complexion, and the pleated skirt accentuating the narrowness of her waist as the material flared out about her shapely calves. She applied a little make-up, and brushed her hair vigorously before she tied it into a knot at the nape of her neck. It added a touch of cool confidence to her appearance, and that was something she desperately needed at that moment. She slipped her small feet into high-heeled sandals to add a few centimetres to her height, and dabbed a little of her favourite perfume behind her ears.

'Where are you going?' Ferdie wanted to know when she found him seated at the kitchen table. In his dressing-gown and pyjamas, and with his face glowing a healthy pink after the bath Salome had given him, Ferdie was not at all that sickly little boy she had placed in Dirk's care a little over a week ago.

'I'm going to see your father,' Alison replied to his query.

'Can I come with you?' he asked eagerly in the process of sliding off his chair, but she placed a restraining hand on his shoulder and shook her head.

'I have to see him alone.' She framed his face with her hands and kissed him on the forehead. 'Be a good boy and stay here with Salome.'

'Will you be long?'

Alison cast a faintly amused glance in Salome's direction, and a tender smile curved her mouth when she returned her gaze to Ferdie's anxious face which was raised to hers. 'I'll be back as quick as I can.'

Alison stepped out into the gathering dusk and walked quickly towards the house where she had once lived with Dirk, and the heels of her sandals dug into the soft grass while her heart beat out a nervous, erratic rhythm. Familiar with Dirk's home, she entered it through the side door, but she paused momentarily in the silent passage to acquaint herself once again with the things she had known and cared for.

Bertrand du Bois still glared down at her disapprovingly, and his wife, Lucille, surveyed Alison with that same sad look which she had wondered about so often. The Persian carpet muted Alison's footsteps as she walked slowly down the length of the passage, and her throat ached at the memory of a happiness which had been marred with the uncertainty of not knowing quite where she had stood with Dirk, but this was not the time to reminisce about the past. Dirk was waiting for her in his study, and, when she stepped into the enormous hallway with its chandeliers and ancient tapestries, she turned towards the first door on her right.

'Come in,' Dirk replied abruptly to her tentative knock on the partly open door, and she took a deep, steadying breath before she stepped into his book-lined study with its comfortable chairs in front of the fireplace where she had spent so many evenings reading while Dirk had sat working behind his desk.

The atmosphere was austere despite the comfortable furnishings, but it was the dark-haired man seated behind the large, polished desk with its littered surface that drew her attention and held it. A black leather jacket fitted snugly across his wide shoulders, and a blue silk shirt was unbuttoned at his strong, sun-browned throat, but the derisive mockery in his narrowed eyes made her back stiffen defensively.

'Punctual as always,' he smiled twistedly.

'And, as always, you make it sound like a crime,' she hit back in an anger that had risen swiftly and sharply within her.

'You misunderstand me,' he pointed out, leaning back in his chair as his cold glance flickered over her where she stood facing him rigidly across the wide expanse of his desk. 'I appreciate punctuality.'

'You have a funny way of showing it!'

'I have no wish to argue with you,' he said, and he sounded suddenly bored as he rose to his feet and walked round to her side of the desk with his hands thrust deep into the pockets of his black suede pants. 'I asked you to come here so that I could discuss business with you and, as I recall, I never mentioned anything about a salary when I offered you this job.'

He towered over her now, dwarfing her with the height and breadth of him, and forcing her to crane her neck to look up at him as he mentioned an amount which was certainly a great deal more than she had received at her previous place of employment. She nodded acceptance, somehow managing to hide her surprise, and only then did he continue speaking.

'You'll start at eight-thirty in the mornings, and

you'll find that there are plenty of preparations you'll have to make before the first batch of visitors arrive at ten-thirty. You'll have a lunch break between one and two, and you knock off at five in the evenings,' he explained her duties while he turned away from her and paced the floor. 'Your weekends and evenings are free except when I'm entertaining guests, and on such evenings I shall expect you to supervise the menu and act as hostess where necessary.'

'I'll manage the latter,' she replied stiffly, 'but do you realise how little I know about winemaking, and you're expecting me to act as your P.R.O. on the estate?'

'I'm well aware of your inadequate knowledge,' Dirk replied with a stinging contempt that made her cringe inwardly, then he picked up a pile of books and thrust them at her. 'You have this evening and tomorrow to study up the subject, and what you don't know you will learn as you go along.'

Her eyes widened incredulously as she steadied the books in her arms. 'You want me to start Monday morning?'

'Naturally.' His chiselled mouth twisted derisively, and those narrowed eyes flashed out a challenge. 'Any objections?'

'None at all,' she replied at once, her back stiffening with anger and resentment. 'I merely asked.'

'There is one other matter I want to bring to your notice,' he halted her when she turned towards the door. 'You may still be my wife legally, but I must warn you not to expect any special privileges because of it.'

So she was to be treated solely as an employee, was she? But hadn't he made that quite clear shortly after her arrival that morning? She failed to see the necessity to underline the matter, but it suited her just fine, and her eyes sparked green fire when she raised her glance to his. 'I didn't come here with the

intention of seeking special privileges, and I want
nothing from you for which I haven't worked.'

Dirk nodded abruptly, the icy fire of his eyes
stabbing at her. 'Now that we've reached an
understanding you may go.'

Her back rigid, and her head held high, Alison
turned once more to leave, but at the door she paused,
and common decency made her say with forced
politeness, 'Thank you for stocking up my kitchen
cupboards.'

'Don't thank me,' he harshly brushed aside the
matter. 'It will be deducted from your first pay
cheque.'

His words had the effect of a sobering slap in the
face. She had been a fool to imagine that his action
had been prompted by a touch of kindness and
consideration, and she felt sick at the thought of her
own naïvety as she walked out of his study clutching
the books he had given her to scour for information.

CHAPTER FOUR

ALISON sat up in bed until late the Saturday evening studying the books Dirk had given her. It made sense, she supposed, to someone who had an above average knowledge of the subject, but the words simply leapt out at her to confuse more than enlighten. Towards midnight her eyelids drooped with fatigue, and she pushed the books aside, stifling a yawn behind her fingers. She switched off the light and was asleep almost the minute her head touched the pillow.

Waking up the following morning in a strange room was rather harrowing. The four-poster bed with its crocheted drapes was large enough for two, but she had shared it with a pile of books, and at the sight of them she was suddenly wide awake. She leapt out of bed and dressed herself quickly, but Ferdie was in the dining-room before her and tucking into a plate of cereal. To Salome's horror Alison wanted no more than toast and coffee, and when Ferdie had gone out to play Alison settled down in the lounge to concentrate on those infernal books Dirk had given her. She had a nasty suspicion that this was part of the revenge Dirk had planned, but she would not give him the satisfaction of witnessing her faltering efforts to grasp the subject matter.

After lunch that Sunday Alison sat once again with her eyes glued in silent concentration to the many pages of small print. Ferdie sat watching her for a time, but he finally became bored, and muttered something about going out to look for his father. Alison let him go without a protest, but by three o'clock that afternoon she was exasperated enough to give up when a familiar voice interrupted her strenuous efforts to absorb what she had read.

'May I come in?'

'Kate, you're an angel,' Alison sighed, pushing her hair out of her eyes as she glanced up at the slender woman who had stepped into the sunny lounge. 'You couldn't have come at a better time.'

'What's all this in aid of?' Kate demanded, astonishment lurking in her eyes as her hand gestured sweepingly towards the array of books which surrounded Alison, and she leaned forward to glance at the titles with some amusement. 'Are you taking a crash course in viticulture?'

'I've only just discovered that winemaking is a very delicate and intricate procedure, and I haven't the foggiest idea how I'm going to explain this briefly to the visitors.' She pressed her fingertips against her aching eyes. 'More to the point, I suppose, is how am I going to get all this information into my head before tomorrow morning.'

'It looks as though you need assistance.'

'I could do with a few helpful hints,' Alison admitted with a tired laugh, letting her hands fall limply into her lap.

'Didn't Dirk explain anything to you?'

'No, he didn't,' Alison replied, getting to her feet to ease the ache in her back. 'He simply gave me these books and told me to study them.'

'Come with me,' instructed Kate after a thoughtful pause. 'And bring a notebook and pencil with you.'

'Where are we going?' Alison queried moments later as she followed Kate's slim figure out of the flat.

'We're going to the cellars.'

'Oh, no, we can't——'

'Oh, yes, we *can*,' Kate interrupted firmly, taking Alison's arm and marching her past the main house towards the cellars. 'Dirk and Rhyno are involved in a lengthy, argumentative discussion about a new cultivar, so he won't even know.'

It felt as if they had entered into a conspiracy against Dirk, but this did not boost Alison's courage when they finally entered the cellars through the arched entrance beneath the carved pediment.

'What exactly do you have in mind?' Alison questioned Kate with a measure of uncertainty.

'I'm going to take you on a conducted tour of the cellar while you make notes, and when I'm finished, you're going to reciprocate by taking me on a similar tour just to get in some practice before tomorrow.'

'That's a crazy idea,' Alison laughed protestingly. 'But I think I like it.'

In a darkened room close to the entrance they found a video machine connected up to a television set, and in the cassette compartment there was a tape which would give the viewer a fifteen-minute documentary on the process of winemaking from the harvesting on Bordeaux right up to the bottling process. It was comprehensive and enlightening, but it also made Alison realise exactly what she was up against. Dirk had offered her a job for which he had known she lacked the necessary qualifications, and it was obvious now that he was not going to lift a finger to help her. He could have had the decency to tell her about the video aid, but instead he had thrust a pile of technical books at her, and she could only surmise that he had hoped she would prove to be a complete failure. Well, she was *not* going to fail, she decided when she eventually followed Kate from the room with her pencil poised above her notebook, and her features were set with the determination which had seen her through the past few years.

'I suggest you let the visitors watch the recorded programme before you take them on a tour of the cellars,' said Kate. 'By that time they'll have a fairly good idea of how things work, and it will make your job so much easier.'

Alison nodded, and after that the educational tour began. Kate explained how the grapes were brought into the cellar and emptied out into the crusher. The worm, a steel spiral roller, destalked and cracked the grapes as it fed them through. It allowed the juice to run freely from the grapes eventually to be pumped into the steel fermentation tanks.

'The free running juice of the white grapes, such as the Riesling, Columbard, and Steen, is used for the better quality wines,' Kate informed Alison. 'The skins are diverted to the press to extract the remaining juice which is tested for its quality. If it's not up to standard, then it's used for a cheap house wine, but if the quality is high then the vintner might decide to add it to the rest of the juice.'

The process for the red grapes, such as the Cabernet and Pinotage, was slightly more intricate, Alison discovered. The skins were pumped, along with the juice, into steel cylindrical fermentation tanks. For approximately four days the temperature was kept between eighteen to twenty degrees centigrade, and this was often accomplished by running cold water over the tanks. The skins would rise to the top of the tank, and this cap would have to be broken and mixed in with the juice from time to time to release the colour pigments in the skins. The white wines were kept at a slightly lower temperature for a few days before they were bottled and left to mature, but the red wines were pumped into wooden vats to mature for anything up to two years before they were ready to be marketed.

Alison made notes, her pencil flying over the paper, and she found herself marvelling at how simple Kate had made it all sound; so simple and interesting, in fact, that even a child could have understood it.

'Now it's your turn to take me on a guided tour,' announced Kate with a twinkle of humour in her sapphire blue eyes as she led Alison back to the crusher where the process of winemaking began.

'I feel like an idiot,' Alison confessed ruefully.

'You will feel even more like an idiot tomorrow if you don't get in a little practise today,' Kate reminded her. 'Simply remember that most of the people you'll be taking through these cellars will know absolutely nothing about the process of winemaking, so they're going to find whatever you tell them informative.'

Alison glanced quickly at her notes, took a deep breath, and tried not to remember that she was taking one of the most knowledgeable women in the field of winemaking on a conducted tour. She stumbled over her words at first, but she gradually gained confidence in herself, and the tour finally came to an end in the cellar with its enormous wooden vats which had been made out of oak imported from the Limousin forests of central France.

'After a sticky beginning you finished the tour like an expert,' Kate gave Alison her honest opinion.

'I've never been so scared in all my life,' Alison confessed shakily.

Kate's laughter was so infectious that Alison laughed as well, but their laughter ceased abruptly when Dirk's harsh voice sliced the musty air in the cellar.

'What's going on here?' he demanded.

Alison's breath caught in her throat as she swung round sharply to see Dirk and Rhyno standing at the entrance to the basement cellar, and something in Dirk's rigid features sent a shiver of apprehension coursing up her spine.

'It was a private little joke,' Kate replied pleasantly before Alison had time to find her voice, but Dirk took no notice of Kate, and continued to direct his icy glance at Alison.

'I don't recall mentioning that I required your services this afternoon to entertain my guests.'

Humiliation robbed Alison of speech, and stained her cheeks a fiery red, but she felt Kate bristling with anger beside her.

'Now look here, Dirk, I——'

'*Kate!*' Rhyno interrupted his wife sharply, and his dark glance issued a warning which, surprisingly, she did not ignore. 'It's time we went home,' he added authoritatively.

The silence was strained when they walked out of the cellar with its musty smell of maturing wine, and Dirk's disapproving glance made Alison feel decidedly uncomfortable as they stepped out into the afternoon sunshine.

In a hurry to get away, Alison turned to Kate and whispered gratefully, 'Thanks . . . for everything.'

'Good luck,' murmured Kate with a wealth of meaning in her voice.

'Nice meeting you again, Alison,' Rhyno said when she turned to leave, and there was a surprising warmth in his steady dark gaze when she placed her hand in his for a brief moment.

Alison nodded, her throat too tight to speak after the humiliation she had suffered, then she escaped to her flat as quickly as possible before Dirk's anger erupted over her head with Rhyno and Kate looking on. It puzzled her that he should have been annoyed at finding her in the cellar with Kate, but this was merely one of the many things she had never understood about Dirk, and now, of course, there would never be a comfortable level of understanding between them.

She was sitting in her lounge, studying the notes she had made, when Salome walked in half an hour later to make an announcement which Alison had vaguely expected.

'Master Dirk wants to see you in his study, madam.'

Alison lowered her gaze to where Ferdie was playing quietly on the carpet with his toys. 'I can guess what it's about,' she sighed.

'I beg your pardon, madam?'

'It's nothing, Salome,' she smiled wanly, rising to her feet, 'and thank you.'

Salome shook her head as she returned to the kitchen and made no attempt to disguise the fact that she was confused, but Alison did not pause to explain as she left Ferdie in the lounge and walked across the lawn towards Dirk's house.

The study door was open, and Dirk was standing in front of the fireplace with his eyes on the empty grate when she paused on the threshold. 'You wanted to see me?' she asked unnecessarily.

'Close the door,' he instructed without looking up, and only when she had done so did he turn to face her, his cold eyes raking over her and making her shiver inwardly. 'There's one thing I would like to make quite clear before we go any further. I don't want you fraternising with my guests unless I order you to do so.'

'But that's ridiculous!' Alison protested, unable to believe that she had heard him correctly. 'Kate and I are old friends, and I think it's quite absurd of you to expect me to ignore her unless you command me to do otherwise.'

'I'm not interested to know what you think, but I want you to make a point of remembering that you're an employee on this estate, and I shall expect you to behave accordingly.'

His words stung like the lash of a whip, but she would not give him the satisfaction of seeing her cringe. 'Are you seriously suggesting that I snub the people I once knew?'

'I'm suggesting that you remember your place, or I might decide that I have no further need of your services.'

'You can't threaten me with dismissal.'

'Can't I?' he smiled coldly and contemptuously. 'For three and a half years you left me in ignorance with regard to the existence of my child. In *my* book, Alison, that was an unforgivable crime, and it leaves me free to deal with you as I see fit.'

'I presume that means you wouldn't think twice about sending me away and never allowing me to see Ferdie again?' she voiced the fear most prominent in her mind.

'Exactly!' he bit out the word savagely, and the colour drained slowly from her face to leave her deathly white.

'You wouldn't be that cruel!'

'Wouldn't I?' He lessened the distance between them, and his ruggedly handsome features were twisted into a harsh, totally unrelenting mask. 'One cruel deed deserves another, don't you think?'

'I was right, then,' she murmured huskily, the icy fingers of fear clamped about her heart, and her eyes dark pools of anguish in her white face. 'You mean to take revenge.'

'Does that surprise you?' he smiled satanically, his lips curling away from his strong white teeth in a way that heightened her fear.

She studied him in silence for a moment, then she gestured helplessly with her hands. 'Do you imagine that I never felt any guilt because of what I did?'

'Guilt?' His hand shot out unexpectedly and bunched into a fist at the back of her head, tugging viciously at her hair so that her head snapped back and she was forced to meet the glittering fury of his glance. 'Do you think that because you've suffered the occasional pang of guilt it's enough compensation for what you did to me?'

'You—you're hurting me,' she protested, her eyes smarting as pain tore through her scalp, but he did not ease his hold on her hair, and she was forced to bite down hard on her lip to prevent herself from crying out.

'I've lain awake these past nights trying to decide what to do about you, but I always end up with only one desire, and that is to put my hands about your throat . . . like this,' Dirk demonstrated, releasing her hair to place both hands about her slender throat. 'And I'd like to squeeze until I've forced every life-giving breath from your body!'

In all her life Alison had never known a moment of terror such as this. She felt his fingers tightening about her throat and she saw the mask of sheer savagery that shifted across his face moments before lack of sufficient oxygen began to blur her vision. She had no doubt that he could kill her without the slightest effort, and the certainty of it was confirmed in her mind as she felt herself driven towards the edge of darkness.

'Dirk . . . for God's sake . . .!' she pleaded, her voice hoarse with fear as she forced the words past the choking pressure of his fingers, and only then did he ease his hold on her throat sufficiently for her to breathe normally, but he did not release her.

'To see you dead at my feet wouldn't give me complete satisfaction either,' he continued as if he were speaking to himself rather than to her. 'No . . . I'll have to find some way to make you suffer, and I want you to go on suffering until you beg for mercy.'

Too numb with terror to attempt an escape, she asked: 'Would seeing me suffer and hearing me beg for mercy satisfy your fiendish desire for revenge?'

'It might.' His hands slid down to her shoulders, and his thumbs moved in an absent, exploratory manner against the base of her throat. 'But then again, it might not.'

Anger smouldered in his eyes, but it was something infinitely more dangerous which was beginning to flow from his hands into her trembling body. It was like a wave of heat surging along fear-chilled veins, and it brushed across taut nerves to create a new tension. At this point she tried to break free, but his left hand grasped a fistful of hair at the base of her skull, snapping her head back, and his right hand slid down to her waist to jerk her up against his rock hard body. She cried out in protest, her eyes stinging with tears, but Dirk's mouth swooped down on hers with a savagery that bruised her lips and forced them apart to lend a certain intimacy to an action which had been intended to hurt rather than arouse.

Her head was spinning as she tried desperately to push him away from her, but when her hands lay flat against his immovable chest she knew the futility of her actions, for the intended punishment had gone awry, and they both knew it as the heat of his body against her own awakened dormant and unwanted emotions. His desire rose fierce and strong, she felt it in the tautening of his thigh muscles against her own, and in the thudding of his heart beneath her palms, but, when that dreaded weakness invaded her limbs, he thrust her away from him with an abruptness that made her stagger momentarily before regaining her balance.

His breathing was ragged, as ragged as her own, but she could not look at him while she stood there trembling with the force of her own emotions. She despised herself, but, when her lowered eyes glimpsed the clenching of his hands as he turned from her, she knew that Dirk despised himself a great deal more.

'Get out of here!' his deep, harsh voice grated along her raw, sensitive nerves, and she fled while her legs were still capable of carrying her from his presence and his house.

Alison felt sick inside when she reached her flat. She had never been confronted with so much hatred before, but Dirk had made it obvious that, despite everything, he still wanted her. The latter should perhaps have elated her, but there was no satisfaction in knowing that she still had the power to arouse that fierce desire in him. It simply flung her mind into a frantic turmoil which left her feeling confused and afraid for herself. It had taken long, seemingly endless months to convince herself that she no longer cared, and it had taken considerably longer before she had considered herself immune, but suddenly she was no longer so sure of how she felt about Dirk.

'What's wrong?' Ferdie wanted to know when she walked into the lounge and found him still on the carpet with his toys.

'Nothing's wrong,' Alison lied, trying to pull herself together. 'Why do you ask?'

He tilted his head at an angle and gazed intently up into her face. 'You look funny.'

She *felt* funny, she had to admit, but it was an odd sort of funny which seemed intent upon driving her to the verge of tears instead of laughter. 'Perhaps I'm just a little tired.'

'You don't look tired. You look . . .' He paused to study her in that peculiar adult manner she knew so well. 'Have you been crying?'

'You heard the madam, *kleinbaas* Ferdie,' Salome intervened sharply, entering the lounge at that crucial point in the conversation, and sensing at once Alison's predicament. 'The madam is tired, and it's time for your bath.'

'Okay,' Ferdie sighed, allowing Salome to take him by the hand and lead him away, but in the door he hung back to glance at Alison over his shoulder. 'You mustn't cry, Mummy. Daddy will look after us.'

His faith in Dirk touched Alison on the raw, and it took every ounce of strength she possessed to control her features, but the moment she was alone she slumped into a chair and buried her face in her hands to smother the choking sob that rose in her throat. *Daddy will look after us.* Oh, God, if only Ferdie knew! She shivered and got to her feet wearily to seek out the sanctuary of her bedroom where she knew no one would disturb her.

She bathed and changed into something warmer before dinner, but no matter how much she tried she could not forget the look on Dirk's face when he had

had his hands about her throat with his fingers exerting that frightening pressure, and neither could she forget the way he had kissed her. Her bruised lips and throat acted as a physical reminder of his savagery, and so also the tenderness of her scalp when she brushed her hair.

It was awkward sitting through dinner that evening and attempting to appear natural in front of Ferdie, and she was relieved eventually when he went to bed so that she could relax comfortably in the lounge with the notes she had made that afternoon. She tried to concentrate on what she had written, but her mind was still too chaotic to take in anything, and she finally got up and went into the kitchen in search of something to drink. She made herself a cup of coffee and sat down at the kitchen table while Salome packed away the last of the dinner dishes. She enquired after the Coloured woman's family, her interest in their welfare sincere, but it was also an attempt to rid herself of her own thoughts.

'Madam,' Salome said as she prepared to leave for her home on the estate, 'it's none of my business, madam, but don't leave Master Dirk again.'

'Why?' Alison asked, lowering her gaze to hide her startled expression. 'What happened when I left?'

'*Die duiwel was los op Bordeaux,*' Salome said fiercely in Afrikaans, her eyes accusing as she shook her greying head wrapped in its colourful turban. 'It was only after Master Dirk gave up trying to find you that things returned to normal, but even then he was never the same again.'

Alison looked up quickly and, against her will, her interest quickened. 'He tried to find me?'

'*Ja,*' Salome nodded adamantly, giving the spotless surface of the cupboard an extra wipe with the cloth before she hung it up on its peg. 'He searched for almost a year.'

It seemed odd to think that Dirk had searched for

her after not having lifted a finger to prevent her from leaving Bordeaux. What had made him change his mind? It could not have been because he cared, could it? *No*, Alison answered her own question. Dirk had never cared for her, but it puzzled her nevertheless why he should have involved himself in such a lengthy search for her.

Alison became aware of Salome watching her intently and, sensing her need for reassurance, Alison said quietly, 'I can't promise that I shan't leave Bordeaux again, but I *can* promise that I will do so only if Master Dirk wishes me to go.'

Salome nodded, a look of relief shifting over her dark face, then she said 'goodnight' and left.

Die duiwel was los op Bordeaux, Salome's words echoed repeatedly through Alison's mind while she sat there alone in the kitchen. *The devil was rampant on Bordeaux!* A wry smile curved Alison's mouth. Dirk in a fury could be compared with the devil himself, and his fury that day she had left the estate had been something too terrifying to remember. Why his fury should have spilled over on to his trusted workers, though, was something she supposed she would never understand.

Alison spent a somewhat restless night mulling over in her mind the things Salome had told her, and she wondered, too, how she was going to cope the following day. Kate had been a tremendous help, but Alison knew that there was a great deal still to learn, and knowing that she could not expect any assistance from Dirk made her feel nervous and edgy. Her chaotic thoughts did not induce sleep and, as a result, she was up early the Monday morning and drinking a cup of coffee long before sunrise.

Apprehensive, but outwardly calm and composed, Alison left Ferdie in Salome's care after breakfast that morning, and walked round to the offices which were housed in the same building as her flat. With no one there to acquaint her with the staff, she had to introduce herself to the two girls who expedited the orders, and she could not entirely blame Connie Hayward and Myrna Cawley when she sensed that they were a little reserved and wary in their approach to her. They had, apparently, been expecting her, and she was promptly shown into the small office which had been set aside for her use. Their assistance was also invaluable in helping her over the first hurdle of the day, but to them she was, annoyingly, the 'boss's wife', and they treated her as such even though they appeared to view the situation with a great deal of speculation. She had, after all, appeared almost out of nowhere after an absence of years, and even though Alison longed to put them at their ease, she knew that it would be unwise to do so if Dirk was to maintain their respect.

The first bus-load of tourists arrived shortly after ten-thirty, and Alison's initial nervousness evaporated swiftly when the visitors responded with interest to what she had to tell them. She silently blessed Kate for her knowledgeable assistance the day before, and she blessed her most especially when she happened to catch sight of Dirk observing her from a distance in the cellars. His presence unnerved her momentarily, but she was determined not to falter and, when she looked again, he was gone.

With her first guided tour of the cellars behind her, Alison directed the visitors towards the tasting lounge where Myrna and Connie assisted her admirably in the task of introducing everyone to Bordeaux wine, and after the tasting session the visitors had an opportunity to place an order, if they wished to do so.

Alison felt tired, but pleased with herself at the end of her first day as P.R.O. on Bordeaux. Several things had happened with which Dirk could have found fault, but she was not going to let the thought of it dampen her spirits. She still had a tremendous amount to learn about the various wines made on the estate, and she was willing to learn all she could, but it would take time.

Her second day as P.R.O. went off a little smoother, and on her third day, when she was returning to her office after a quick lunch, she bumped into Mike Petzer. Tall and lean, with laughing blue eyes, and sun-bleached hair, he extended a friendly hand towards her.

'Welcome back, Alison,' he said in his gravelly voice.

'Thank you, Mike,' she smiled up at him, her hand disappearing into his and remaining there quite naturally. 'How are you?'

'Very much married these days.'

'So I've heard.'

'I've been away for a few days or I might have called on you sooner, but I hope you'll come over to my house some time to meet Erica, my wife,' he invited, his manner pleasant and natural as if she had never been away, and her heart warmed to him as it had done four years ago when she had come to Bordeaux as a bride.

'I'd like very much to meet your wife.'

'Here comes the boss,' he ended their conversation abruptly, releasing her hand as he glanced beyond her. He might have looked wary, she could not be sure, but that ready smile was still on his lips, and he winked characteristically as he murmured, 'See you some other time.'

He walked away briskly, taking the path towards the vineyards, and only when he was out of sight did she turn slowly to face the man approaching her. She felt no alarm at the sight of Dirk, but something in his expression warned her that this was not going to be a pleasant encounter. He reached her side a moment later, his hand warm and rough as he gripped her arm tightly above the elbow and ushered her out of the sun into the cool, thatched-roofed building. Myrna and Connie's curious glances followed them into Alison's office, but Alison was more aware of that sudden erratic beat of her heart when Dirk closed the door behind him to shut them off from the others.

This was the first time they had come face to face since the Sunday afternoon in his study when he had kissed her so savagely. No matter how much she tried, she could not thrust from her mind the memory of those moments in his arms, and she thought of it now as he stood facing her in the confined space of her office. Tanned and intensely male, he still had the power to stir her senses alarmingly, and she put the width of her small desk between them for comfort while she waited for him to speak.

'I presume you know that Mike is married?' he broke the strained silence between them, and she felt herself go rigid with distaste at the accusation hidden behind that query.

'You presume correctly.'

'Erica is in the final stages of pregnancy, and I wouldn't want her unnecessarily upset about anything.'

His voice was low, like the rumble of a threatening storm, and his manner suggested something once again that made her voice cool with suppressed anger when she spoke. 'Your concern for Erica Petzer is commendable, I must say, but she has nothing to fear from me, and neither do I deserve a lecture from you for simply being friendly with Mike.'

'There'll be no need for me to lecture you if you remember to keep your association with him friendly ... and nothing more,' Dirk warned, his eyes narrowed and filled with naked hostility.

Alison bit back the angry words that rose to her lips, and decided wisely it would be safer to change the subject. 'I'm sure this can't be the only reason you wanted to see me privately.'

His threatening attitude eased a little, but his eyes were still cool and dispassionate as they flicked over her small slimness in the emerald green woollen dress she had bought the previous winter. 'I'm having seven people over to dinner this coming Friday evening, and I want you to supervise the menu and act as hostess.'

'Am I correct in assuming that when you require my services as hostess it doesn't necessarily mean that I'll be dining with you?' she questioned in an attempt to know more clearly where she stood.

'Your assumption is correct.'

Having her suspicions confirmed did not afford her the relief she had imagined it would; it hurt deeply, and anger was her only weapon against it. 'Am I to behave like a glorified servant, then?'

'That's what I pay you for,' Dirk stated bluntly, and the hurt became a sword that drew blood as she looked into those cold, expressionless eyes observing her.

They faced each other in silence, two strangers who had once been lovers, and as the antagonism piled high between them she somehow managed to hide from him the success he had had in his objective.

'May I have the names of your guests in order to place them at the dinner table?' she asked in a calm, businesslike manner that surprised even herself and, picking up her notebook and pencil, she waited in silence for him to begin.

'I've invited the Andersons and the De Wits from the adjoining farms, and also the Bassons from Paarl.'

Alison knew Fred and Ivy Basson. She had lived with them during those weeks prior to her marriage to Dirk, but this was not the time to reminisce about the past.

'That's only six people,' she reminded Dirk.

'Yvette Paulson will be the seventh.'

'I should have guessed that, I suppose,' she remarked with only barely concealed bitterness as she kept her eyes lowered to her notebook to hide the pain that shot through her. 'Yvette was never left out of anything that went on here at Bordeaux, and it appears the same situation still exists.'

'And why shouldn't it?' Dirk demanded harshly, a forbidding note in his voice.

'No reason at all, and I was simply thinking aloud,' she brushed aside his query as she added Yvette's name to the list, and she silently congratulated herself on the steadiness of her hands while her insides felt as if they had been bundled into a quivering mass of pain. It was totally ridiculous to let it affect her in this way, but, for the moment, there appeared to be nothing she could do to subdue her feelings. 'Any preferences as far as the menu is concerned?' she asked.

'None,' he said abruptly, his mouth twisting derisively when she happened to glance up at him. 'Except, of course, that the meal lives up to Bordeaux standards.'

There it was again, that hidden threat in his voice that said quite clearly, 'Try anything funny, and you're out!' She was imagining it, perhaps, but there was no longer a scrap of doubt in her mind that Dirk intended making life on Bordeaux as difficult as possible for her.

'I shall do my best.'

'I shall accept nothing less,' he warned darkly.

Alison could still feel his presence in her small office long after he had gone, and it made her squirm inwardly. She could not imagine why she was allowing him to hurt her in this way. She was no longer the inexperienced girl he had married, but a woman of twenty-four with a mind of her own. It had taken her a long time to build up a certain confidence in herself. Why, then, was she allowing him to walk all over her in this way? And why did he still have the power to hurt her?

CHAPTER FIVE

DINNER that Friday evening was an event which Alison viewed with trepidation. She had discussed the menu with the kitchen staff, selected some of Bordeaux's best wines, and most of the dishes had been prepared under her watchful eyes, but she still felt nervous and edgy about it. Working all day, as well as seeing to the preparations, had been tiring, but she had thrived on it, for it had given her little time to think about anything else. When she paused that evening to study herself in the mirror, however, she found herself wondering anxiously whether the dinner would be to Dirk's satisfaction.

The black dress she chose to wear accentuated the golden texture of her skin, and the material clung softly to her small breasts and slim waist. For practical reasons she had tied her dark hair into a shapely knot at the back of her head, and her reflected image in the mirror looked calm and sophisticated, but inwardly she was quaking with nerves.

Ferdie had been bathed and was in his pyjamas and dressing gown when Alison entered the kitchen. Salome turned from her inspection of the stew, and her frowning glance made Alison say quickly, 'You may put my dinner in the oven, Salome, and I'll have it later.'

'I can't understand, madam, why you are not having dinner with Master Dirk this evening,' Salome persisted in angry confusion.

'I told you, Salome,' Alison smiled a little cynically, 'I shall be there as a hostess, and not as a guest.'

'But, madam——'

'And please see that Ferdie goes to bed at the usual time,' Alison cut into Salome's protests.

'Can't I stay up a little later tonight?' Ferdie wanted to know with a vaguely petulant look on his face.

'I want you in bed at seven as usual, and that's an order.'

'Oh, *gee*, Mummy!' he wailed.

'No arguments,' she warned before he could say more and, kissing him lightly on the forehead, she left to fulfil her duties as Dirk's hostess.

It was a cool evening, and she welcomed the warmth of Dirk's home when she stepped into the dining-room with its stinkwood and yellow-wood furniture. Her critical glance skimmed the table, checking on the silver laid out on the white damask cloth with its matching table napkins. The candles were in the candelabra, ready to be lit before dinner commenced, and the flat oval-shaped arrangement of bright yellow chrysanthemums added a splash of colour to the decorative table.

Alison wondered vaguely where Dirk was, but she had too much else on her mind as she crossed the hall and walked quickly towards the spacious kitchen to check that everything was in order. The prawn cocktails were in the refrigerator, ready to be served, and Alison was hastily assured by the staff that the succulent lamb roasting in the oven would be done on time. Fresh vegetables simmered in the pots, and the warm, spongy dessert with its baked apple filling had been prepared and placed in the warming oven with the cinnamon sauce. The red wines had been decanted earlier that day to enliven them and to allow the sharper odours to escape in order to make them velvety smooth on the palate.

The doorbell chimed and Alison glanced agitatedly up at the clock on the kitchen wall. Six-thirty! The first guests had arrived, and she walked quickly into the hall to welcome them as was expected of her.

Dirk stepped into the hall while she was relieving the De Wits and the Andersons of their coats. Their curious glances had disturbed her, but Dirk's presence disturbed her to the point that her heart bounced uncomfortably in her breast. Dark, forceful, and ruggedly handsome in an evening suit, Alison caught herself staring at him momentarily like a star-struck teenager, but her lapse fortunately went unnoticed as Dirk welcomed his guests and took them into the living-room for a drink before dinner.

'Pull yourself together!' she warned herself sharply as she turned to deposit the armful of coats on the old-fashioned stand in the hall, and she had barely done so when the doorbell chimed once again.

This time it was Fred and Ivy Basson. Middle-aged, warm and friendly, they had obviously known that she would be there, and their expressions mirrored a genuine pleasure at renewing her acquaintance. Pleasure made way for surprise, however, when she had hung up their coats and was gesturing them into the living-room.

'Aren't you joining us?' Ivy Basson wanted to know, looking totally bewildered when she realised that Alison had no intention of accompanying them.

'I'm here only in a working capacity for the sake of my son's health,' Alison explained her position briefly and uncomfortably.

'But——'

'Ah, you've arrived,' Dirk's voice interrupted Ivy Basson's protests, and Alison was almost relieved when he took them off her hands and ushered them away to join the rest of his guests.

The only one still to arrive was Yvette, but Alison knew from past experience that Yvette never arrived anywhere at the stipulated time. She had always been late to make what could only be termed as a spectacular entrance, and this evening was no exception. Alison hovered agitatedly between the kitchen and the spacious hall, and ten minutes passed before the chime of the doorbell heralded Yvette's arrival.

She was even more beautiful than Alison had remembered. Beneath the white fur cape her hyacinth blue evening gown accentuated the curves of her tall, shapely body, and deepened the colour of her large grey eyes. Her raven black hair was swept up on to her head in a stylish manner which drew attention to her slender throat where an expensive diamond and sapphire necklace sparkled in the light from the chandelier overhead. That familiar yet incredible air of innocence still seemed to hover about her, but the words that spilled from her lovely mouth were, as always, pure venom when they were directed at Alison.

'So you've come crawling back again,' she remarked caustically. 'I wonder how long you'll stay this time?'

Alison bit back a sharp retort and forced a pleasant smile to her lips. 'May I take your cape?'

Yvette's attention was already elsewhere as she let her fur slide from her shoulders into Alison's waiting hands.

'Dirk, *darling*,' Yvette exclaimed softly, gliding quickly across the floor into Dirk's waiting arms, and Alison froze on the spot as Dirk lowered his dark head to brush his lips against Yvette's ivory-skinned cheek.

It was like watching a replay of something which had happened long ago. Yvette was standing in the circle of Dirk's arms while he smiled tenderly down into her upturned face, and suddenly all the old feelings Alison had buried so carefully seemed to rise within her with a shuddering force.

'I'm glad you could make it, Yvette,' Dirk was saying, one arm still draped about Yvette's waist as they turned towards the living-room.

'You know I never ignore an invitation when it comes from you,' Yvette replied provocatively, tilting her head so that it lay briefly against his shoulder.

Dirk made use of this opportunity to direct his glance at Alison, and his eyes mocked and challenged her to say something, but, even if she had wanted to, she was too stunned to react, and her face had become set in a rigid mask behind which she hid the feelings storming through her.

Moments later, alone in the hall, Alison discovered that she had clutched Yvette's cape so tightly that her fingers ached, and she turned to hang it with careful haste on the hook. The familiarity of that subtle perfume which clung to the fur seemed to twist that non-existent sword in her heart, and she was forced to recall the afternoon she had arrived home from the doctor with the news that she was pregnant. Yvette's perfume had lingered in the hall that day, and Alison had followed the scent like a retriever into Dirk's study to find Yvette in Dirk's arms with her dark head resting intimately against his broad chest. Alison could recall standing there paralysed into a state of questioning uncertainty, but Dirk's eyes above that elegant head had merely taunted her into believing the worst.

The memory of it all flashed through Alison's mind as if it had happened the day before instead of four years ago. She had waited, hoping against hope for some sort of explanation, but none had been forthcoming, and she had fled to her room, leaving them in the study with their arms presumably still wrapped about each other. Later, when she had lowered herself to demanding an explanation, Dirk had erupted into a stubborn fury which had solved nothing, and which had finally resulted in Alison leaving Bordeaux. This was not the time to recall the agonising experiences of the past, Alison knew that, but somehow she had been incapable of preventing the memories from flooding back like a tide rushing in, and it had brought with it all the feelings she had succeeded in suppressing for so long.

It took a moment to pull herself together, but it felt as if it had taken an eternity before she was sufficiently in command of herself to return to the kitchen, and she took care to remain there until it was time to light the candles in the dining-room and announce that dinner would be served.

From a culinary point of view the evening was an outstanding success, but for Alison there was a personal agony involved which sliced deep into her soul. It hurt not to respond as she would have wished when the Bassons tried to engage her in conversation as she served the various dishes, and it hurt every time she encountered Dirk's open hostility, but somehow she managed to remain outwardly calm and composed.

The conversation at the dinner table was pleasant, but the atmosphere was not without a certain amount of strain. Alison had never met the De Wits and the Andersons, and they were clearly curious about her presence there in Dirk's home that evening, but the Bassons were curious for a totally different reason. To them she was Dirk's wife, regardless of the estrangement, and their eyebrows were almost constantly raised at the manner in which Dirk charmed Yvette while Alison had to fetch and carry from the table.

'You do very nicely as a servant,' Yvette's honeyed voice remarked cuttingly when Alison finally wheeled in the trolley with the coffee. 'Mind you, Alison, I never considered you had potential for very much else.'

The conversation stilled around the table, and for endless seconds it seemed as if Dirk's guests were almost too afraid to breathe while their expressions ranged from intense curiosity to annoyance. With everyone's attention centred on her, Alison felt like someone who had been dragged, unprepared, on to a stage. The eyes focused on her seemed to expect a performance of some sort and, with humiliation still stinging her cheeks, she chose retaliation as her act. If Yvette wanted to behave like a cat, then she would be treated as such.

Clinging desperately to the calm front she had presented all evening, she picked up the silver milk jug and, selecting a saucer from the tray, she turned towards Yvette to ask innocently, 'Would you like some milk?'

The jibe found its mark and, eyes flashing, Yvette leapt to her feet amid the sound of smothered laughter which came from everyone except Dirk.

'How dare you!' she spat out the words like a vicious snake, and Alison had visions of being physically attacked, but Yvette turned instead to the granite-faced Dirk who had risen from his chair. 'Are you going to allow her to insult me like this?' she demanded shrilly.

The cold fury in Dirk's eyes scorched Alison as he brushed past her to place his hands gently on Yvette's shoulders. 'I shall deal with her later,' he spoke soothingly, and Alison could almost see the bristling anger drain out of Yvette until that wild look left her eyes. 'Sit down and calm yourself, Yvette,' he said quietly, urging her back into her chair.

No one spoke while Alison poured their coffee, but she happened to glance at Fred Basson to see him wink at her with distinct encouragement, and after that the conversation was slowly resumed.

Alison was not proud of her own behaviour, and a lead weight settled in her chest to remain there for the rest of the evening. When Dirk's guests began to depart shortly after ten o'clock that evening, Alison was there to give them their coats and bid them goodnight, but Yvette still lingered in the living-room. Dirk could see her out himself, Alison decided and, casting a final critical glance at the spotless kitchen, she let herself out of the back door and walked briskly into the cold night air to where the light in her lounge beckoned.

Salome put away her embroidery when Alison walked into the kitchen, and her eyes questioned

Alison's pinched expression, but on this occasion she respectfully said nothing. She simply took Alison's dinner out of the oven and placed it on the kitchen table before she said goodnight and went home.

Alison sat down and rested her elbows on the table as she stared at the plate of food. The stew looked and smelled appetising, but she was too tense to eat even a mouthful at that moment. Her head felt heavy; so heavy that she lowered it on to her hands and sat there staring with unseeing eyes at the steam rising from the dinner Salome had kept for her. She felt depressed, confused, and emotionally exhausted. The strain of the past few hours was something she would not have wished on her worst enemy, and with it all there was Yvette's stabbing remark which seemed to echo repeatedly through her tired mind.

You do very nicely as a servant. Mind you, Alison, I never considered you had potential for very much else.

It had been a spiteful, wounding remark which Alison had not deserved and, instead of reprimanding Yvette, Dirk had calmed her with a surprising gentleness which had left Alison feeling like a criminal because of her retaliation.

Why? Why had he allowed Yvette to ruin their marriage, and *why* was he still pampering and protecting her as if she were something precious?

The kitchen door was thrust open and Alison looked up sharply to see Dirk's large bulk, still in formal dress, framed in the doorway. As he closed the door behind him and approached the table his icy glance travelled from her swiftly controlled features to the untouched plate of food in front of her. He was in a savage mood, she could see it in the way he moved and in the set of his jaw. He had said he would deal with her later for daring to hit back at Yvette, but somehow Alison had not expected him to carry out his threat quite so soon.

Nervousness drove her to her feet like a schoolgirl

confronted by the headmistress, but her voice was cool and tainted with unaccustomed sarcasm when she asked: 'I hope everything was to your satisfaction?'

'Everything except the way you behaved towards Yvette,' he accused harshly, and without delay.

'Did you expect me to ignore her nasty remarks?'

'She was my guest.'

'And what am I?' she demanded furiously and foolishly.

'You're a paid servant, as Yvette so rightly pointed out.'

Alison had been put in her place before, but this time Dirk's words stung with an acid that made her flinch visibly. His method of revenge was despicable, but it was effective in a way she had never imagined.

'You could have divorced me and married Yvette,' she said without actually intending to, and his eyes glittered with anger and something else which she could not define. 'Why didn't you, Dirk?'

'I would have been quite within my rights to divorce you, but it's suited me to remain married.'

'You mean, I suppose, if you can get what you want in the present circumstances, then why bother with divorce?' she questioned scathingly, but this time the dark fury in his rugged face told her that she had gone too far.

'Mind your tongue, you little vixen, or I might forget that you're the mother of my son, and throw you out!' he threatened as he towered over her menacingly, but Alison had gone beyond the point of curbing her tongue.

'Thank you for crediting me with *some* status, at least, above that of your servant.'

The silence between them seemed to crackle with electricity, and Dirk's large hands gripped the back of the kitchen chair until his knuckles whitened with the obvious effort of preventing himself from striking her, or something worse.

'I will warn you for the first and the last time,' he said in a dangerously quiet voice. 'Be careful how you behave towards Yvette in future, or you might live to regret it.'

Alison could not explain even to herself what she felt at that moment as she stared up into his hooded eyes. 'Is she so very important to you?'

'Yes, she is.'

There had been no hesitation, or complementary pause for thought, just a simple affirmative, and it had cut her to the quick.

'I understand,' she murmured huskily, lowering her lashes to hide the look of stark misery which had entered her eyes.

'Daddy?' a small voice from the inner door broke the strained, agonising silence, and it made them swing round to see Ferdie standing there in his striped pyjamas and his dark hair tousled.

'Hello, son,' Dirk said easily while Alison still made a desperate attempt to find her voice. 'Why aren't you in bed and fast asleep?'

'I was asleep, but I woke up and heard you talking to Mummy,' Ferdie explained, venturing further into the kitchen on his bare feet.

'Would you like a glass of milk?' Alison finally asked, attempting to sound natural.

'No, thank you,' Ferdie shook his head.

'Then it's back to bed again, my lad,' ordered Dirk, picking him up and striding firmly towards the door.

'Mummy?' Ferdie questioned over Dirk's broad shoulder. 'Are you coming too?'

'Yes, of course,' she said, hastily coming to her senses.

Alison followed Dirk's tall figure down the dimly lit passage and, together, they put Ferdie to bed and kissed him goodnight. It felt strange this feeling of unity she experienced; almost a sense of belonging, but she realised sadly that they had no future together as a family unit. There was no place for her in Dirk's life other than the one she was occupying at that moment, but saddest of all was the painful, unquestionable discovery that she still loved this man with his heartless, sometimes cruel ways, and she loved him at that moment with a burning tenderness when she saw him smile at Ferdie. If this was how Dirk felt about Yvette, then she owed him an apology, if nothing else.

'We'll have to be a little more careful in future what we say to each other when Ferdie's about,' he said when they walked into the kitchen some minutes later, and she nodded absently.

'Dirk . . .' Words, apologetic and meaningful, froze on her lips when those cold eyes met hers, and she was forced to fall back on to that well-worn apology, 'I'm sorry . . . I really am.'

His jaw hardened and those big hands clenched at his sides as if her apology had angered him, then he strode out of the flat, leaving her there to face her cold plate of food, and an even colder feeling in her heart.

Knowing how she still felt about Dirk made life that much more difficult for Alison on Bordeaux. She was being paid an astronomical salary, but as the weeks passed she realised that Dirk intended her to work like a veritable slave for every cent. Her weekdays were occupied with taking visitors on a tour of the cellars and, regardless of the weather, the scheduled bus-load of tourists would arrive twice daily on Bordeaux to sample the estate wine and to learn the intricacies of winemaking.

Alison was not surprised that she was learning more about wine as time went by, but so also was her job expanding to the extent that she found herself attending meetings and wine auctions as well as interviewing prospective customers and taking charge of the advertising. It was an enormous and sometimes frightening task for Alison, who had so little experience in this direction, but Connie and Myrna were a tremendous help once their initial wariness of her had dwindled. When Dirk did not require her to act as hostess to his many friends and associates, she spent her evenings preparing for the following day, and quite often she would not get to bed before midnight.

There was only one reason why she found her arduous task worthwhile, and that was the fact that Ferdie appeared to be flourishing in this climate. Since her arrival on Bordeaux he had had only one mild attack of asthma, and that had been on a cold, misty day when it had seemed as if the sea air was blowing directly inland into the valley. Alison had heard that familiar rattling in Ferdie's chest when they had sat down to lunch that day, and when darkness descended she had found herself sitting beside his bed administering the medication Dr Samuels had prescribed. She had watched Ferdie more closely after that incident, but nothing happened as they drifted into midwinter, and he changed slowly from a tired, listless little boy into an energetic, boisterous bundle of mischief.

There was very little opportunity to pursue a social life of her own. She had met Mike Petzer's wife, Erica, but it had been during a brief visit shortly after the birth of their baby girl, and the only time she was able to see Kate and Rhyno was when they came to Bordeaux.

'This is ridiculous!' Kate exploded one evening when she slipped away from the party to join Alison in the kitchen. 'Your place is there inside with the rest of us, and not here in the kitchen at the beck and call of all and sundry, and how you tolerate Yvette's snide remarks is simply beyond me!'

'Please, Kate,' Alison warned softly, darting a nervous glance at the door for fear of Dirk walking in on this discussion. 'I appreciate your concern, but this is what I'm paid to do, and I'll do it even if it kills me.'

Kate's eyes became smouldering blue flames of anger. 'I never imagined Dirk could behave in such a sadistic, vengeful manner!'

'I hurt him badly when I left him and never told him about Ferdie,' Alison defended Dirk at once.

'And what about your own hurt?' Kate demanded incredulously. 'Doesn't that count at all?'

'There's so much you don't understand, Kate.'

'You can say that again,' Kate announced dryly. 'I've seen Yvette insult and humiliate you right under Dirk's very nose, and I've seen you take it without a murmur. *Why*, Alison? Why do you let her do this to you, and why does Dirk allow it?'

Alison avoided Kate's probing blue glance and stared helplessly down into the plate of small savoury tarts on the table in front of her. 'Yvette's happiness is important to Dirk.'

'Does her happiness mean so much to him that he can stand there and do nothing about the way you're being humiliated?' Kate asked with that familiar directness. 'For God's sake, Alison, you're his wife!'

Alison swallowed convulsively at the tightness in her throat. 'When I walked out on him I forfeited the right to his concern.'

'I don't believe it!' Kate exclaimed incredulously.

'What don't you believe, Kate?'

Dirk had entered the kitchen with a stealthy silence that had caught them unawares, and fear and love clamoured simultaneously in Alison's breast at the sight of him, but Kate was undaunted by his presence as she rounded on him furiously.

'I don't believe it's right that you should treat your wife in this abominable manner in front of all your associates and friends,' she stormed at him before Alison could prevent her. 'The way you thrive on Alison's humiliation is quite revolting to witness, and it's time someone had the guts to tell you so!'

A frightening silence followed Kate's outburst until Dirk drew himself up to his full, imposing height, and there was anger as well as irritation in the way he moved his wide shoulders beneath the perfect cut of his black suede jacket.

'I'll thank you not to interfere in something which doesn't concern you, Kate,' he announced autocratically.

'It does concern me when I see a friend of mine being insulted the way you allow Alison to be insulted,' Kate replied coldly and, not at all intimidated by him, she turned to face Alison. 'I think it's time Rhyno and I left, so I'll say goodnight.'

Without so much as a cursory glance in her host's direction, Kate marched out of the kitchen and left Alison to face Dirk alone.

'I'm sorry, Dirk,' Alison managed at length to break the explosive silence between them, and her hands fidgeted nervously with the apron she had tied about her waist. 'Kate doesn't understand, and you must forgive her.'

'I take it you were crying on her shoulder about the treatment you've been receiving,' he accused with characteristic harshness.

'I did nothing of the kind!'

'What prompted that little scene, then, may I ask?' he demanded derisively.

'I told you, Dirk, she—she doesn't understand.'

He was towering over her suddenly, his hands at her throat, and his thumbs beneath her chin tilting her face up to his as he growled, 'I sometimes don't understand my own reasoning. I could have saved myself a tremendous amount of irritation and frustration by simply taking Ferdie, and sending you to hell where you belong.'

There was so much hatred emanating from him that

Alison wanted to weep. *She* had done this to him, she could lay the blame at no one else's door, and at that precise moment she came close to hating herself intensely.

'Oh, here you are, darling,' Yvette's honeyed voice made him drop his hands to his sides and step away from Alison. 'We've all been wondering what could have happened to you.'

'A slight problem arose that needed straightening out,' Dirk replied smoothly as Yvette slipped her arm possessively through his.

'Been slipping up on the job, have you, Alison?' Yvette queried, her smile venomous and the sweetness of her voice tinged with acid.

Dirk's short bark of laughter as he led Yvette away simply added insult to the injury and, seething with anger, Alison's fingers curled about the plate of savouries. She felt an intense desire to hurl the plate across the kitchen in an attempt to ease her frustration, but she curbed it swiftly and took a deep, steadying breath, then she plastered a smile on her unwilling lips and carried the plate of savouries out of the kitchen.

Kate and Rhyno were leaving as Alison entered the crowded living-room. Dirk and Rhyno were shaking hands as if nothing had happened, but Kate gave Dirk an icy stare which might have made a lesser man shrivel, but Dirk merely lifted a faintly amused eyebrow. They were, at least, not parting as enemies, and Alison felt relieved even though she appreciated Kate's concern for her.

The party continued until the early hours of the Saturday morning, but Alison left shortly after eleven when Dirk indicated that she would no longer be needed, and she escaped thankfully to her cosy flat where the fire still burned lustily in the grate when she went into the lounge.

Too tense to think of going to bed, she changed into her night attire and curled up in a chair in front of the fire. She had selected a book to read, but it remained unopened on the table beside her chair as she sat staring into the crackling log fire and felt the heat of the dancing flames on her face. Dirk had expressed the desire to send her to hell on several occasions, but there was no need for him to send her into that particular furnace. She was in a private hell of her own making where pain, desolation and despair were her constant companions and, as she mentally listed the mistakes she had made in the past, she found herself less inclined to want to blame Dirk entirely for their disastrous marriage. She had been young and foolish, and she had perhaps expected too much.

Alison sighed heavily into the silence and closed her aching eyes as she leaned back in her chair. She could understand and accept her present reasoning, but what she could never understand or accept was Dirk's involvement with Yvette Paulson. What was so secretive about their relationship that he could not have told her, his wife? Was it love that drove them so constantly into each other's arms? If it was, then why, in heaven's name, had he not married Yvette?

Tears burned behind Alison's closed eyelids and forced their way through her long, thick lashes to slide down her cheeks. She did not make an attempt to stop them; she felt too tired suddenly to lift a finger, and she simply sat there while the hot tears paved their way down her cheeks. It was idiotic to cry; tears had never solved anything, but as the minutes passed she had to admit that they were relieving the tension and the frustration which had been building up in her all evening. She would have given anything at that moment to be back in her flat in Cape Town. She had had a comfortable life devoid of all the tension and misery she was experiencing now, but it was futile to look back. She had to face the future, and the future looked blacker than the starless night outside.

It was long after midnight before Alison left the

warm fireside to crawl into bed, but her dreams that night were fraught with visions of Dirk's angry features at her frustrated attempts to vindicate herself. He was going to make her suffer, he had threatened to do so and—*dammit*—he was succeeding!

CHAPTER SIX

THE sun had barely risen over the Klein Drakenstein mountains when Alison was awakened by the sound of someone entering her bedroom. She opened her eyes a fraction to see Ferdie approaching her bed. He was dressed in his favourite blue jeans and checked shirt, and he walked on tiptoe, but when he saw that she was awake he clambered up on to the bed beside her.

'Aren't you going to get up this morning?' he asked with childish disgust, and he looked so much like Dirk at that moment that Alison was instantly on the defensive.

'It's the first morning in weeks that I have the opportunity to stay in bed a little late.'

'Salome is making your favourite cheese omelette for breakfast,' Ferdie told her persuasively.

'I suppose that means I shall have to get up,' she smiled, stretching against the pillows and stifling a yawn behind her hand.

'Yes,' Ferdie agreed excitedly, bouncing up and down on the bed. 'Get up, get up, get up!'

'Oh, what did I do to deserve this?' Alison moaned humorously, then she pulled him down beside her and they wrestled playfully in a way they had not done for ages.

'I love you, Mummy,' he said unexpectedly when their laughter had ceased, and he wrapped his arms tightly about her neck.

'I love you too,' she responded fervently, hugging him close to her and running her fingers lovingly through his short dark hair.

'I love my daddy too,' he said, pulling a little away from her to stare up at her with something close to wariness in his eyes.

'I'm glad,' she whispered, her throat tightening.

'Do you love Daddy too?'

The question came as something of a shock, and she was rendered speechless for a moment, then she gathered her wits about her and said carefully, 'How I feel about your father is something I don't want to put into words right now, so why don't you go and wait for me in the kitchen while I get dressed?'

'Okay.' He wriggled out of her arms and slid off the bed, but when he reached the door he turned to glance at her. 'I like staying here on the farm.'

Alison sat there in bed for a while after he had left, and she found herself wondering what had prompted that last remark. Was it possible that he had settled down so swiftly in his new environment that he was afraid she might uproot him again, and take him away from the father he had learned to love? There was no chance of that, of course, but there was every chance that Dirk might tell *her* to go. What then? she wondered. Would Ferdie be happy to stay on without her?

She shut her mind to these depressing thoughts, and half an hour later, when she walked into the kitchen to join Ferdie for breakfast, she was dressed warmly in beige slacks and a thick emerald green sweater. She enjoyed these moments alone with Ferdie, and she always made the most of them. Heaven knew, these moments were becoming more infrequent as time went by. Dirk had been a demanding husband, but he was considerably more demanding as an employer. She worked long hours during the day, and quite often until late at night when Dirk required her services. He was totally relentless where she was concerned, but she was determined that he would never hear her complain.

This was the first Saturday she would have to herself since arriving on Bordeaux, and when Ferdie went out to play, she found a notebook and pencil and sat down to draw up a list of the items she required in town. The list was long, but she had almost completed it when the telephone Dirk had had installed some weeks ago started ringing in the lounge.

'Oh, no!' she thought despondently. 'Don't tell me Dirk has found something for me to do on my very first weekend off!'

No one could have missed that ring of annoyance in her voice when she finally answered the telephone, and Kate's voice was instantly apologetic.

'Have I interrupted something important?'

'No, you haven't,' Alison laughed with relief. 'I was afraid it might be Dirk, and I was preparing myself to do battle.'

'Talking about Dirk,' said Kate, 'I shot my mouth off last night, and I apologise for it. I ought to be trying to help you, but instead I've made it worse, and I——'

'Kate, please,' Alison interrupted hastily. 'You said what you did because you're my friend, and because you care. I appreciate that.'

'I wish I could forgive myself that easily,' Kate seemed to groan at the other end, then she changed the subject. 'Are you free this afternoon?'

'So far, yes.'

'What about coming along for tea and a chat? God knows I see you seldom enough.'

'Thanks, I'd like that,' Alison accepted the invitation.

'Wonderful!'

Alison returned to the kitchen a few moments later to complete her shopping list, but her mood was much lighter now than it had been before, and she was actually humming softly to herself when she finally drove into Paarl with Ferdie seated beside her in the Renault.

It was a warm, sunny winter's morning with not even a wisp of cloud in the sky, and Kate could almost forget her problems as she waded through her shopping list and bought a few items of clothing for Ferdie, who had grown out of everything lately. They rounded off the morning in a tea room, and, as Alison sat watching Ferdie emptying the plate of cream scones, she found it difficult to believe that this was the same child she had nursed through those many agonising hours while he had fought for breath. Gone was the pale, thin, and listless child, and in his place was a tanned, healthy-looking boy with bright eyes and rosy cheeks. He had grown sturdy and energetic, and, despite the circumstances of their arrival in Bordeaux, Alison felt a tremendous gratitude towards Dirk for this remarkable change in their son.

Their son. There it was again, those words that made of them a family unit, but, sadly, it was not like that at all. They were no longer a family unit, and the blame for that was hers as much as Dirk's.

They arrived back at Bordeaux shortly before lunch, and Salome came out to help Alison carry the parcels into the flat. The scones and tea had diminished Alison's appetite, but Ferdie sat down to lunch and emptied his plate regardless of the amount of cream scones he had devoured that morning.

'Put on a clean shirt and wash your face and hands,' Alison told him when he finally pushed back his plate and slid off the chair. 'We're going to visit Aunty Kate at Solitaire.'

'I can't go,' Ferdie announced as he followed Alison into the lounge, and she turned sharply to frown down at him.

'What do you mean, you can't go?'

'I'm going into the vineyards this afternoon with Daddy.'

'Oh,' said Alison, feeling slightly winded by this disclosure.

'You can come too,' Ferdie issued the invitation with a childish certainty that Dirk would welcome her presence, but she shrank from the idea.

'No, I don't think so,' she replied slowly, swallowing down her disappointment. 'I still think, though, that you should put on a clean shirt and wash your face and hands.'

'Oh, do I really have to?' Ferdie scowled up at her.

'Do as your mother tells you, Ferdie,' Dirk spoke unexpectedly from the outer door which Alison had left open to admit the fresh, sweet-smelling valley air.

'Yes, Daddy,' said Ferdie, obeying his father at once, and marching out to do as he was told without another murmur.

'We're in the throes of pruning the vines to prepare them for a new growth, and I want to check on the shoots which have been newly grafted,' Dirk explained when she had mastered her feelings sufficiently to face him. 'Ferdie will be quite safe in the truck with me.'

'I know,' she replied, trying to ignore the masculine appeal of his tall, muscled frame in those familiar khaki pants and shirt. 'Ferdie has grown very fond of you.'

She wished she had not said that when she saw his eyebrows rise above eyes that gleamed sardonically. 'Does the thought displease you?'

'Not at all,' she said, turning away from him with some annoyance. 'A boy needs a father he can love and respect.'

Outside she could see the trees stirring in the breeze, but inside of her Alison felt something else stirring to life during the ensuing silence as Dirk came up behind her. His hands were heavy on her shoulders, his touch burning her through the silk of her blouse, and her pulse quickened in response to his nearness.

'A boy also needs his mother,' he said severely, turning her to face him, but Ferdie chose that moment to return, and Dirk's expression revealed nothing behind that rigid mask she had come to know since returning to Bordeaux.

'I'm ready, Daddy,' announced Ferdie, his eyes going from one to the other, and Dirk's hands fell away from Alison's shoulders to leave her feeling vaguely bereft.

'Come along, then,' he ordered, taking Ferdie by the hand.

'I'm going to drive out to Solitaire this afternoon,' Alison announced almost as if she expected Dirk to have something to say about it, but he merely acknowledged her statement with a curt nod as she followed them out to where he had parked his truck, and a few moments later she was standing there alone, watching the dust settle which had been churned up by the truck tyres.

Bordeaux was an exceedingly beautiful estate, but the tension was always piled so high that Solitaire took on the appearance of a tranquil oasis that afternoon when Alison had tea out on the terrace with Kate. Eloise sat on a blanket surrounded by her toys, gurgling happily in the warmth of the winter sun, and Alison felt curiously at peace.

Kate's conversation revolved, quite naturally, around the activities on the estate. She took an active interest in everything which concerned Solitaire, and Alison found herself learning more about viticulture without actually intending to. The pruning of the vines was a delicate operation on which the new season's growth depended, and then there was also the need for a good rainfall during the late winter and early spring months. A dry, hot season could raise the level of the sugar in the berries, and this was not always so desirable from a vintner's point of view.

The discussion inevitably turned to Dirk when Kate said: 'I know this is none of my business, Alison, but how much longer can you continue working under the present circumstances?'

'For ever, if I have to,' Alison replied determinedly. 'I don't want to lose Ferdie.'

'Dirk reminds me in some ways of my father,' Kate remarked, her eyes reminiscent as she stared out across the garden towards the vineyards in the distance. 'My father never appreciated having his decisions queried, and he seldom chose to explain his actions. He not only expected but *demanded* complete trust from those close to him, and that made it difficult for strangers to understand him.' She laughed, and it was a vexed, faintly amused laugh as she returned her level gaze to Alison's still form in the chair close to hers. 'There was a time when even I didn't understand his reasoning.'

'That sounds like Dirk,' Alison smiled sadly, absently stretching out a hand to steady Eloise when she teetered on her chubby legs. 'Not even when our marriage was at stake would he unbend his rigid principles a fraction to explain.'

'Didn't you trust him?'

'I did at first, but . . .' she sighed and gestured helplessly with her free hand, 'trust needs to be nurtured like everything else, and my trust began to wane when I continuously found Yvette ranking all over him. When I questioned him about it, it would end up in an unsatisfactory argument, and my suspicions mounted up until the barrier between us was too solid to break down.'

'There has to be a simple explanation for it somewhere,' Kate insisted with some annoyance.

'There is,' Alison admitted with a cynical twist to her lovely mouth. 'He cares more for Yvette than he ever cared for me.'

'I simply can't and won't believe that,' Kate exploded with visible distaste.

'There's no other explanation that I can think of.' Alison shrugged her shoulders with a forced casual-ness in an attempt to hide the pain that was clawing at her insides, then she swiftly changed the subject to one which lay close to Kate's heart. 'Eloise has grown tremendously since I first saw her.'

'And she's the apple of her father's eye,' Kate laughed, lifting the chubby little girl on to her lap and removing the soggy biscuit from Eloise's hands to wipe them with a paper handkerchief. 'Rhyno says she has my vile temper and his steel determination, and that's quite an electrifying combination!'

'You are happily married, aren't you, Kate?'

'Yes, of course I am.' Kate looked up, somewhat startled. 'Why do you ask?'

Uncomfortable suddenly beneath Kate's direct gaze, Alison brushed a non-existent crumb from her skirt and felt compelled to finish what she had started so unintentionally.

'There were rumours, I believe, that you'd been forced to marry Rhyno.'

During the ensuing silence Alison glanced up to see the sparks of anger flaring in Kate's blue eyes, but the anger was soon replaced by an oddly rueful expression.

'I *was* forced into marrying Rhyno,' Kate's disclosure shocked Alison. 'My father's will insisted upon our marriage if I wanted to inherit Solitaire, and I hated my father for it almost as much as I thought I hated Rhyno at the time.'

'You thought you hated Rhyno?' Alison prompted curiously.

'It was resentment, actually,' Kate explained, returning Eloise to the blanket where the toys lay conveniently scattered, and pouring a second cup of tea for Alison and herself before she resumed her explanation. 'I'd always believed that I would one day take over the management of the estate, but my father was of a different opinion, and he engaged Rhyno as estate manager on Solitaire and La Reine. I was attracted to Rhyno from the very first moment I saw him, but my resentment overruled all other feelings until I believed I despised him—and then there was also the disclosure in my father's will that La Reine had once belonged to Rhyno's mother.'

'That wasn't a very good basis on which to start any sort of marriage,' Alison remarked with something akin to horror.

'No, it wasn't,' admitted Kate, amusement dancing in her eyes. 'Resentment and suspicion seldom make a good basis for a marriage, but Rhyno was remarkably patient with me.'

'You managed to overcome the barriers between you, though,' Alison supplemented with some envy.

'Only when I came to my senses sufficiently to admit to myself that I'd used my resentment as a weapon to ward off the happiness which was mine for the taking. Oh, God!' Kate's eyes looked bleak suddenly as she recounted a painful memory. 'I'll never forget how I felt when my waspishness made Rhyno retaliate one night by saying that I possessed none of the qualities he admired in a woman. That really shook me.'

She looked so stricken that Alison was instantly filled with remorse. 'I'm sorry, Kate.'

'Please don't apologise,' Kate smiled a little wanly 'It does me good to delve into the past occasionally. I can look at my mistakes objectively and, I hope, learn from them.'

Those words remained with Alison when she drove back to Bordeaux late that afternoon. Perhaps, if she delved into the past, she could look at her mistakes objectively and learn from them. But was that not exactly what she had been doing ever since Dirk had stormed into her life once again?

The cypress and oak trees were casting long, deep shadows across the lawn when Alison approached the homestead and parked her Renault. The light was on in her lounge and smoke was curling from the chimney jutting out from the thatched roof. It was a welcoming sight, and she pulled her coat more firmly about her to keep out the biting cold of the approaching night as she walked along the gravelled path. She entered her flat—only to stop abruptly, her heart leaping into her throat when she found Dirk and Ferdie sprawled on the carpet in front of the fireplace with a toy train circling lazily on its tracks between them.

'Mummy, Mummy, come and look!' Ferdie cried excitedly, jumping to his feet and darting across the room to tug at the sleeve of her coat where she stood frozen at the sight of her often austere husband winding up the clockwork engine so that it could resume its senseless circling. 'Daddy fixed the engine for me,' Ferdie informed her, his eyes shining with admiration when he glanced at his father.

'That's nice,' Alison managed lamely, closing the door to shut out the cold just as Salome walked into the lounge.

'Are you staying for dinner, Master Dirk?'

'Please, Daddy,' Ferdie underlined Salome's invitation. 'Please stay and have dinner with us.'

Steel-grey eyes met Alison's and she did not miss the challenge in their depths as she swallowed nervously. 'You're welcome to stay, if you like.'

Dirk's eyes held hers a moment longer, then he got to his feet and turned to face the Coloured woman hovering expectantly near the door. 'Thank you, Salome, I'll stay for dinner.'

His acceptance came as something of a shock. He had challenged Alison into inviting him to stay, but she had never believed he would accept, and her hands shook visibly when she took off her coat and draped it across the back of a chair.

'Dinner will be ready in half an hour,' Salome announced, a strangely triumphant smile on her face as she walked out of the room.

'Put away your train set, and have your bath before dinner,' Dirk instructed and, much to Alison's surprise, Ferdie obeyed without a protest.

'I'm afraid I haven't so much as a glass of wine to offer you before dinner,' she apologised nervously the moment they were alone, but Dirk solved the problem characteristically.

'You get the glasses and I'll fetch the wine from the cellar at home.'

Her legs were shaking after he had gone, and she sat down on the arm of a chair for a brief moment to steady herself before she went in search of two glasses. Her hands were still not quite steady when she wiped the glasses carefully, and she had barely returned to the lounge when Dirk returned with a bottle of vintage Steen.

Alison was as tense and awkward as a teenager on her first date, and her attempts at making polite conversation were almost tragic when the things she really wanted to say had to remain locked for ever in her heart. The glass of wine she had before dinner eased some of her tension, but Dirk's male presence was intensely disturbing until he steered the conversation towards his plans to export Bordeaux wine through the Stellenbosch winery. She observed him closely throughout dinner, listening attentively while he elaborated on the various aspects of viticulture, but her truant mind wandered eventually until she found herself simply watching the play of expressions on his ruggedly handsome features while he talked. Alison was not alone in her observation of Dirk. Ferdie was also watching him intently, admiration shining in his wide eyes as he listened to the deep rumble of Dirk's voice, and a lump rose in Alison's throat as she noticed again the striking resemblance between father and son.

'Oh, God!' she groaned inwardly. 'How much more of this can I tolerate without making my feelings obvious?'

Salome took Ferdie off to bed after dinner while Dirk and Alison retired to the lounge with their coffee, and once again that awkward tension settled between them. Dirk leaned back in his chair in front of the fire, and stretched out his long legs until his feet almost touched the grate. It awakened old memories of evenings spent like this in companionable silence, but on those occasions she had sat on the floor at his feet with her head resting comfortably on his knee instead of sitting so rigidly tense in a chair some distance from him.

'More coffee?' she asked, attempting to break the silence between them, and he looked up sharply from his brooding study of the leaping flames in the grate.

'No, thanks.' His eyes glittered mockingly, the firelight accentuating the hollows and planes of his handsome, but austere features, and her heartbeat quickened when his glance travelled slowly over her in a way that made her feel as if she was being stripped down to her skin. 'It's quite like old times sitting here in front of the fire with you, but it's the wrong fireplace, and the wrong passage in time.'

Alison's hand was remarkably steady when she placed her empty cup on the small table beside her chair, and uneasiness drove her to her feet so that she stood gripping the mantelshelf with her fingers until her knuckles shone white through the skin. It was as if he had read her thoughts, and his remark triggered off that spark of pain inside her which she had been trying to suppress. She shivered despite the heat of the fire against her body, and when she spoke her voice was slow but distinct.

'Our marriage was a mistake.'

She heard him get to his feet, and the deep timbre of his voice directly behind her made her nerves react violently. 'Are you hinting that you want a divorce?'

'Wouldn't that be preferable to living the way we are?' she asked, remaining with her back to him for fear that he might see the utter desolation in her eyes.

'The day I put this ring on your finger I sealed our fate,' he told her in an ominous sounding voice as he prized her left hand free of the mantelshelf and twisted the ring about her finger. 'You will remain my wife until the end of our days.'

'Forever is a long time to live the empty lives we're living now,' she argued softly, staring down at her small hand resting in his rough palm, and his fingers curled in a punishing grip about hers.

'The choice was yours, Alison, and you chose to walk out on the life we had together.'

'I don't deny that, but——'

'Go on,' he prompted when she paused to reflect the past.

'You never gave me much reason to believe that our marriage stood a chance,' she confessed, finding it increasingly difficult to think straight while he was standing so close to her.

'Our marriage stood as much chance as anyone else's, but not when it came up against your suspicious mind and petty jealousy,' Dirk accused harshly, releasing her hand to grip her shoulders, and he turned her roughly to face him.

'All I wanted was to understand, but you refused me an explanation, and when I questioned you, you behaved as if I'd done something criminal,' she pointed out, schooling herself before she raised her eyes to meet his icy gaze. 'It was only natural that suspicion and jealousy should follow.'

His mouth twisted derisively. 'Suspicion and jealousy don't make a good marriage.'

'I know that, but you expected too much, Dirk.' Her gaze fell before his to become riveted to the opening of his blue shirt where the dark chest hair curled tightly against his tanned skin. The desire to press her lips against it was so intense that she trembled and continued to speak in a nervous rush. 'You wanted me to trust you; to believe blindly that your association with Yvette was purely platonic. Can you blame me for thinking the worst when you refused to explain why I nearly always had to find you in each other's arms? Did you honestly expect me to stand aside and say nothing while she was fawning all over you in that possessive manner?'

That was not at all what she had intended to say, but she knew it was too late to retract it as she saw the blaze of fury in his eyes. 'I told you then that you could think what you damn well pleased!'

'And the same applies now, I take it?'

'Precisely!'

Bitterness welled up inside her, but when she raised her eyes to his she found herself trapped in a vacuum of longing from which there was no escape. The tremor in the hands that gripped her shoulders and the darkening of his eyes told her that, despite everything, he still wanted her, and there was nothing more she wanted at that moment than to lose herself in his arms, but she knew she dared not risk it.

'I think you'd better go,' she whispered huskily, attempting to move away from him, but he anticipated her actions, and she was caught up against him with a fierce swiftness that made her breasts hurt against his hard chest.

There was no time to speak before his mouth descended on hers with a force that drove her lips apart. His kiss was an insult spiked with a mixture of anger and desire, and the way his hands roamed her body was degrading rather than arousing. Alison struggled against him, but there was no escape from the prison of his arms until he was ready to release her, and when he finally did, she felt too sick and dizzy to do anything except to stand there swaying before him with her wide, reproachful eyes fastened on to his.

'Thanks for the dinner,' he smiled, but his smile was no more than a satanic twist of his lips, and the memory of it remained with her long after he had gone.

'Oh, God,' she groaned softly, sinking into the chair behind her and burying her white, distraught face in her hands. 'What did I do to deserve this?'

It was a silly question. She knew very well what she had done. She had questioned his integrity, and she had injured his pride, but most of all she had robbed him of the joy of watching his son's growth from birth. The latter alone was unforgivable, but, combined with the others, it clearly spelled out a disastrous future. Worst of all was the realisation that there was nothing she could do about it; nothing except to do as as she was told, and to accept in silence whatever came her way.

Alison worked harder than ever during the following weeks. She was up most mornings before dawn, and seldom got to bed at night before twelve. The original dining hall of the old homestead had been used as a storage room in which mostly old crates had been stored, but Alison had it cleared out with Dirk's permission. The walls were whitewashed, and the yellow-wood floor was restored to its original gleaming brightness before tables and chairs were brought in. As a spacious tasting room it was ideal, and it would allow the visitors to Bordeaux to relax with a glass of wine while they watched the video programme at the start of each tour.

Every spare moment she had was spent drawing up pamphlets and order forms. She had them printed, and finally sent them off to the various centres for distribution. It had been an arduous, time-consuming task, but it began to pay off dividends when the orders came in thick and fast for Bordeaux wine.

'I can't imagine why no one thought of paying more attention to the advertising side of the business before,' Myrna Cawley remarked one morning when she was sorting through the huge batch of orders which had arrived in the post.

'The rise in the popularity of Bordeaux wine ought to make Mr du Bois smile for a change,' Connie Hayward added laughingly, winking mischievously at Alison before she settled down to her own batch of orders.

Alison did not reply to this as she went through to her office to sort through her own correspondence, but she doubted very much if anything she did would ever make Dirk smile with genuine pleasure, and an involuntary sigh passed her lips when she picked up the letter opener and slit open the first envelope.

Among her post there was a card from Dr Samuels which said briefly, 'It's time for Ferdie's check-up. Come see me Friday the 27th at ten-thirty. I shall keep an hour free for you.'

Alison studied her desk calendar. Friday the twenty-seventh. 'That's tomorrow!' she realised with something close to dismay. She would have to speak to Dirk about giving her the day off, but she dreaded having to confront him about anything other than work.

That evening, after dinner, she lifted the receiver of the telephone in her flat, and pressed the required button which would connect her with the main homestead.

Dirk answered almost at once with an abrupt, 'Yes?'

'May I please come and see you for a few moments about something important?' she asked servilely.

'I'll be in my study,' he announced, and a decisive click at the other end left her holding a lifeless instrument which she dropped into place almost as if it had stung her.

If he was in that kind of mood, then she did not hold out much hope for herself when it came to asking a favour of him.

The nights were still chilly with spring on the doorstep, and Alison tightened the belt of her thick woollen jacket as she stepped out of her flat and walked the short distance to Dirk's house. The moon was full and it lit her path with a silvery glow, but she was too busy rehearsing what she had to say to notice the beauty of the star-studded sky. The cold, too, made her insides shake . . . or was it nerves?

'*Damn!*' she muttered to herself, quickening her pace in agitation. She felt like a schoolgirl about to ask permission to miss a lesson instead of a woman wanting to consult her husband about something which concerned them both.

Husband. The word stood out from the rest as if it had been lit with neon tubing. Technically, or legally speaking, Dirk was her husband, but she could no longer think of him as such after all the intervening years. He was now her employer, and not a very accommodating employer at that, but they still had one thing in common which bound them together whether they wanted it or not. Ferdie was a growing bundle of mischief and childish arrogance, but he was the child she adored from the moment of his birth, *and* he was Dirk's.

Her palms were damp with undisputed nervousness when she entered the house and walked down the dimly lit passage towards Dirk's study. The door stood open, and he looked up when she walked in. On the desk lay a document which she recognised instantly as the tentative sales figures for the month which she had hastily drawn up that afternoon for his customary inspection, and she wondered anxiously what he thought of it.

'What can I do for you?' he asked bluntly, gesturing her with a wave of his hand into the vacant chair on the opposite side of his desk, and she lowered herself into it hastily when she felt her knees begin to shake beneath her.

'May I have the day off tomorrow, please?' she asked with equal abruptness, and totally at a loss as to what she had intended to say in order to lead up to that request.

'Why?'

'Why?' Alison repeated, startled out of her wits by his hostility and her own diversion from her well-rehearsed speech, but she pulled herself together smartly when she glimpsed the impatient tightening of his mouth. 'I'd like to take Ferdie to see Dr Samuels in Cape Town,' she explained.

'Has Ferdie been ill?'

'No,' she assured him hastily when she glimpsed a recognisable flicker of concern in his otherwise cold eyes. 'I'd promised Dr Samuels that I would bring Ferdie to him for a check-up after three months, and I received a card from him today to tell me that he's made an appointment for tomorrow at ten-thirty.'

'This Dr Samuels,' said Dirk, his eyes narrowed and intent upon her face as he leaned back in his chair. 'Was he your doctor when Ferdie was born?'

'Yes, he was.'

Alison shifted uncomfortably beneath that thoughtful, steely gaze during the silence that followed her affirmative reply, and the silence stretched to unbearable lengths before he said curtly, 'You may take the day off.'

His tone of voice implied dismissal, and she sighed inwardly with relief as she rose to her feet and murmured shakily, 'Thank you.'

'Alison,' that deep-throated voice stopped her before she reached the door, and she turned to see Dirk pick up her handwritten statement. He gestured vaguely with it, his face expressionless and giving her no indication what to expect, and she pushed her trembling hands into the pockets of her jacket when he began to speak. 'You've done a tremendous job as P.R.O., and you've succeeded almost in doubling the sales of Bordeaux wine.'

A compliment from Dirk was as rare as fungus on a treated vine, and she stared at him speechlessly for some moments before she was able to compose herself sufficiently. 'The superior quality of your wines warranted a bigger sale, and I'm glad you approve of what I've done.'

Afraid that he might follow this up with a snide remark to spoil the unexpected compliment, she murmured a hasty 'goodnight', and returned to her flat.

The beauty of the moonlit night once again went unnoticed as she struggled to cope with that flutter of hope in her heart. Dirk had complimented her. *So what!* her cynical mind jeered. It was still a far cry from what she yearned for, and dreams and hopes were so seldom realised.

CHAPTER SEVEN

LEONARD Samuels' waiting-room was reasonably full when Alison sat down in a comfortable chair and made room for Ferdie to squeeze in beside her. They were half an hour early for their appointment, but, while Ferdie found himself a children's magazine to page through, Alison relaxed in her chair and allowed her thoughts to wander to the incident which had occurred early that morning before her departure from Bordeaux.

Dirk had been out on the warpath, she had heard him in the packaging room, verbally tearing apart one of the farmhands for something which she had considered a totally minor offence, and she had felt herself shrinking inwardly at the fierceness of that thundering voice.

Salome had stood beside Alison's car shaking her head, and although she had said nothing, there had been a distinct accusation in her eyes when her glance had met Alison's.

'Did I do this to him, Salome?' Alison had asked confusedly without actually realising she had spoken. 'Is it my fault he's become such a fierce and difficult man to please?'

Salome had lowered her gaze servilely, but when she replied she contradicted her attitude. 'The day you move back into the main house with Master Dirk is the day that this part of the valley will echo again with laughter. It has been better since you and *kleinbaas* Ferdie have come to stay, but a man needs his woman like the vineyards need the sun and the rain, and I say that with respect, madam.'

She had walked away, obviously neither wanting

nor expecting a reply, and Alison had driven to Cape Town with Ferdie. Now, as Alison sat there waiting to see Dr Samuels, Salome's words ricocheted through her mind until they became a confusing jumble which made no sense at all. A man needs his woman? The valley will echo with laughter? Salome must surely have her facts wrong. It was Yvette whom Dirk needed to that extent.

'Alison, my dear, it's good to see you again,' Leonard Samuels smiled when she finally entered his consulting-room, and he kissed her on the cheek like a long-lost friend before he stood back and eyed her critically. 'You've lost weight, if I'm not mistaken.'

'I've been working hard,' she shrugged off his remark, while the nurse took Ferdie through to the examination room.

'I hope your husband is treating you fairly?' he persisted.

'He treats me well enough.'

'Does he have a good relationship with Ferdie?'

'They have a very good relationship,' she smiled, feeling as though she had trod on to safer ground. 'They're almost inseparable these days.'

'Good,' nodded Dr Samuels, standing aside for her to precede him into the examination room. 'Well, let's have a look at you, young man,' he smiled at Ferdie, tickling him in the ribs where he lay on the examination table, and making him shriek with laughter.

The examination was thorough and lasted several minutes while Alison looked on in silence. She studied the doctor's expression in an attempt to see what he was thinking, but, as always, he gave nothing away until he had completed his examination.

'Remarkable,' he said at length, smiling broadly as he pushed his stethoscope into his coat pocket and stepped back from the table. 'There's been a vast improvement, Alison. His lungs, in fact, sound disgustingly healthy ... if you will forgive the expression.'

'Then it's all been worthwhile,' she whispered unsteadily, her eyes brimming with tears, and only then did she realise how tense and anxious she had been.

'Help the child with his shirt, Sister, and keep him occupied for a while,' Leonard Samuels instructed hastily, then Alison felt his arm about her shoulders, and she was being guided out of the room. With the interleading door closed he lowered her into a chair, and placed a large handkerchief in her hands when he saw her searching vainly for one in her handbag. 'Dry your tears, Alison.'

'It's silly of me to cry,' she admitted with a shaky smile when she had managed to control herself. 'I'm sorry.'

'Alison ... my dear, is there no chance of patching up your marriage?' Leonard asked, seating himself on the corner of the desk.

'None, I'm afraid,' she sighed, unable to look at him.

'Is it because you no longer care for your husband?' he questioned, rescuing his handkerchief before she ripped the fine linen between her agitated fingers.

'It's Dirk who doesn't care,' she lowered her guard at last. 'He's so bent on revenge that he frightens me at times, and added to that I am still faced with the old problem for which there appears to be no solution.'

With no one else to turn to, and no one who cared, Alison had confided in the kindly Leonard Samuels during those months before Ferdie's birth. It was not necessary now to elaborate, and he instantly grasped her vague reference to Yvette.

'Dirk is still associating with that woman?'

'Yes.' She swallowed down the rising lump in her throat and gestured helplessly with her hands. 'Oh, it's all so impossible! Dirk lives by such a rigid code of strange principles that it makes it impossible for me to understand him, and there's even less chance now of having a sensible, enlightening discussion with him.'

'Revenge may be sweet at first, but it tends to be bitter when it recoils on one,' the doctor observed wisely. 'Perhaps, when he has discovered this, he might be more willing to unbend a little.'

'I hope so,' Alison sighed, 'but at the moment I can't visualise the possibility of Dirk unbending to the extent where he would be absolutely honest with me.'

'Have *you* always been totally honest with him?'

'I've always been as honest as I——' She paused abruptly, arresting herself on the verge of telling a lie as certain incidents in the past flashed through her mind to mock and rebuke her.

'You were saying?' prompted Leonard, dragging her thoughts back to the present, and her gaze was a little startled when she raised it to his.

'Dirk accused me the other evening of having been suspicious and jealous, and I didn't deny it. During those months we lived together I *did* become suspicious and jealous, and anger had been my only defence against those despicable feelings. As a result, I suppose, I never quite made him understand that I wasn't accusing him of having an affair with another woman, and that I was simply questioning him in a desperate attempt to understand the relationship that existed between them.'

'You never explained this to him after you'd both had time to calm down?'

'I couldn't have explained it even if I'd wanted to.' Her eyes looked haunted as she delved back into the past. 'He'd withdrawn from me mentally to such an extent that he'd become totally unapproachable, and I finally left matters as they were in the hope that it would all sort itself out.'

'You were at fault, then, as much as he was,' Leonard pointed out calmly but bluntly.

'Yes,' she confessed, looking a little startled at having admitted the truth, but bitterness soon took over. 'This soul-searching is all very well, but it still doesn't explain why my husband's home *and* his arms are always open to receive Yvette Paulson.'

Leonard Samuels could give her no satisfactory answer to that disturbing question. Dirk was the only one who could do that, but she was afraid of hearing the truth. Once, in a moment of anger, Dirk had hinted at his feelings for Yvette, but Alison could not bear to hear him actually say that he loved her.

Alison was in no hurry to get back to Bordeaux. She went shopping for a few personal things, and took Ferdie to lunch at a restaurant in Sea Point from where they could watch a few people braving the calm but icy sea. It was a cloudy but surprisingly warm day, and at that particular moment she had to admit to herself that she missed not living in this beautiful city nestling at the foot of the majestic Table Mountain.

It was almost four o'clock that afternoon when they arrived back at Bordeaux. Alison parked the Renault and she was still in the process of collecting her parcels when Dirk's truck pulled up next to them.

'What did the doctor say?' he demanded, getting out of his truck and slamming the door in characteristic fashion.

'The doctor said I'm disgustingly healthy,' Ferdie forestalled Alison in such an adult manner that both she and Dirk burst out laughing.

Alison sobered swiftly, however, at the sound of that deep-throated laughter coming from Dirk, and she found herself staring in fascination at the transformation in his normally harsh features. Laughter made him look strangely young, and he was so incredibly handsome at that moment that her heart was beating erratically against her ribcage.

When his laughter subsided he affectionately ruffled

the boy's short dark curls and asked: 'Are you coming with me for a drive down into the vineyards?'

'Yes, please,' Ferdie accepted the invitation enthusiastically, and he opened the door of the truck and climbed into it without anyone's assistance.

Dirk's face was an inscrutable mask once more as he inclined his head briefly in Alison's direction, then he followed Ferdie into the truck and slammed the door.

'I'll have him back in time for his bath,' said Dirk though the open window, and moments later she was standing there alone. His laughter had been so fleeting that she could almost believe it had never happened, but she found herself wishing he would laugh more often.

This part of the valley will echo again with laughter, Salome's words flashed unbidden through Alison's mind, and she sighed heavily as she turned and went into the flat.

'Mummy, may I have a cake for my birthday?' asked Ferdie one Friday evening while he sat in the kitchen sampling the biscuits Alison had taken out of the oven.

'Your birthday isn't for a long time yet.'

'I know,' he nodded, biting into his fourth biscuit, 'but may I have a cake with candles on?'

'Yes, of course you may.'

Discussing birthdays was a serious matter to Ferdie, and Alison had to hide a smile as she placed the last baking tray in the oven, but she was unprepared for the question that followed.

'When is Daddy's birthday?'

The smile on her lips froze and she straightened abruptly, her glance darting involuntarily towards the small calendar against the side of the wall cupboard. 'It's next week Thursday,' she heard herself answering him hesitantly.

'How old will he be?'

Alison did a swift mental calculation. 'Thirty-six.'

'*That* old?'

'Thirty-six isn't old,' she argued with a mixture of amusement and annoyance.

'I want to buy Daddy a present,' Ferdie finally voiced what she had begun to fear.

She could imagine what Dirk would think when Ferdie confronted him with a gift on his birthday, and she shivered inwardly with fear and distaste. 'I don't think you ought to——'

'Oh, *please*, Mummy?' Ferdie interrupted her hesitant refusal, and when she looked down into his wide, anxious eyes she knew she could not burden him with her own fears and problems.

'We'll take a drive into town tomorrow morning and see what we can buy him,' she capitulated.

'Yippee!' he exclaimed excitedly, and helped himself to yet another biscuit before she put him to bed.

Alison was convinced she had made the wrong decision, but it was too late now to change her mind, and she would simply have to ride whatever storm arose from this incident.

They went to town the following morning as she had promised Ferdie, and they spent almost an hour in a gift shop while he darted from one interesting item to the next. Alison was determined neither to assist nor encourage him, and he finally selected a gold pen he felt certain his father would like. His small face glowed with excitement and anticipation when he held out his choice towards Alison, and a glimpse at the price almost took her breath away, but she paid for it without a murmur when she envisaged Ferdie's disappointment.

'If you want this to be a surprise, then you'd better not tell your father about the present you've bought him,' Alison warned Ferdie when they eventually drove back to Bordeaux.

'I won't tell him,' Ferdie promised and, small as he was, she knew that he would keep his secret well.

Spring moved stealthily into the valley, and the sap rose in the vines until tender young leaves were sprouting in the vineyards. The gentle August rains had soaked the fertile soil as if in preparation for the new season, and on the morning of Dirk's birthday the warm September sun shone down on an earth which was showing signs of new life everywhere.

The dew was still heavy on the grass outside when the sound of an approaching truck made Ferdie jump up from the breakfast table.

'There's Daddy!' he cried, darting out of the kitchen.

'Ferdie, wait!' Alison tried to stop him, but he had already crossed the lounge and flung open the front door.

She attempted once more to detain him, but Dirk had already seen Ferdie careering across the lawn towards him and, moments later, Alison stood biting her lip nervously as she watched Ferdie take his father's hand literally to drag him towards the flat.

Alison felt her heart hammering against her ribs at the sight of that tall, khaki-clad figure. He smiled indulgently as he allowed Ferdie to lead him inside and, quite suddenly, he was dominating the small lounge with the sheer height and breadth of him. His stabbing glance met hers searchingly where she stood observing the proceedings with an outward calmness which belied the frightening turmoil within her, then Ferdie captured his attention.

'I have a present for you,' Ferdie said proudly, taking the gift out of the writing desk's drawer and holding it out towards Dirk. 'Happy birthday, Daddy.'

Alison held her breath while Dirk stared down at the small parcel which Ferdie had wrapped rather untidily. He smiled as he accepted the proffered gift, but Alison could see that the smile did not reach his eyes.

'Thank you very much, Ferdie.'

'Aren't you going to open it?' Ferdie demanded excitedly, unaware of the tension which was building up rapidly in their comfortable lounge, and Dirk obliged him by carefully stripping away the gaily coloured wrapping.

'This is exactly what I needed,' Dirk announced as he lifted the pen from the cushioned recess of the rectangular box to study it intently, then he looked down into his son's glowing face, and once again that mirthless smile curved his mouth. 'I'll use it every day.'

He lifted Ferdie high in his arms, and the child laughed delightedly as he locked his arms about his father's strong neck, but over Ferdie's shoulder Dirk's cold eyes stabbed at Alison until an iciness began to trickle slowly through her veins.

'You haven't finished your breakfast, *kleinbaas* Ferdie,' Salome announced unexpectedly from the doorway.

'I'm not hungry,' Ferdie pouted with a stubbornness he had inherited from his father.

'If you want to go for a ride in the truck with me, then you'd better finish your breakfast, my lad,' Dirk announced severely as he lowered Ferdie to the floor.

'Okay,' Ferdie agreed docilely, and Salome ushered him out of the lounge, closing the door behind them.

The room seemed to shrink instantly in size, and a near-claustrophobic tension gripped Alison as she found herself facing Dirk alone. In the tree outside the window a Cape canary sang loudly and shrilly, shattering the silence and jarring her nerves to the point where she almost flinched visibly.

'Don't use Ferdie in an attempt to make things easier on yourself,' Dirk's quiet, menacing voice accused her of the very thing she had been afraid of.

'I don't know what you're talking about,' she replied with a pretended innocence as she met the stabbing fury of his gaze.

'I'm talking about this!' He virtually thrust the pen

under her nose, and she backed away from him instinctively. 'It was your idea, no doubt?'

An angry denial sprang to her lips, but she suppressed it almost at once when Leonard Samuels' query leapt into her mind. *Have you always been totally honest with him?* A blunt denial would serve no purpose at that moment. Only the truth would suffice.

'To Ferdie a birthday is an important and exciting event. He was discussing, prematurely, what he wanted for his birthday in November, and this led to him asking about your birthday. When I told him it would be today, he insisted on buying you a present, and I didn't dissuade him. I admit that I paid for it, but the choice was his entirely.' Her grey-green gaze was cool, and her voice had a miraculously calm ring to it, but underneath the surface there was a simmering anger she could not suppress. 'I could have talked Ferdie out of it, I suppose, but I saw no reason to let the existing circumstances between you and me spoil his enjoyment, and if you want to make something of that, then you're welcome,' she stated coldly, brushing past him and walking out of the lounge.

Alison did not stop until she reached her office, and it was only then that she realised how much she was shaking. She lowered herself into her chair, thankful for these few minutes alone before Myrna and Connie arrived, and it took all of that time to compose herself sufficiently. She was studying her diary when the two girls came into their office, and she was once again her calm, smiling self when they looked in on her to say a cheery 'good morning'.

'We have a busy schedule ahead of us today,' Alison warned them. 'There are two bus-loads of tourists arriving this morning, and there will be another two this afternoon. I'm told they're eager to spend their money, so sharpen your pencils, and have the order forms handy.'

Connie and Myrna groaned in playful protestation,

and lingered a while for a friendly but businesslike discussion, but the preparations began in earnest when they returned to their office.

Alison did not see Dirk again that morning, and neither did she see him during her lunch hour. That afternoon, however, she was in the darkened tasting room where the visitors were watching the video while they sipped their wine, and she was so engrossed in what she was doing that she paid no attention when the door was opened behind her, but her breath caught in her throat when a heavy hand gripped her shoulder.

'Take over, Connie,' Dirk quietly issued the instruction to the girl who had chosen to assist Alison with the afternoon tours. 'I want to talk to my wife.'

Alison had no idea what could be so important that she had to be called away from what she was doing, but she refrained from questioning Dirk until they faced each other in her office.

'Is something wrong?' she asked when he closed the door to allow them some privacy, and her thoughts leapt at once to Ferdie.

'Will you have dinner with me this evening?'

The invitation was so unexpected that it succeeded momentarily in driving the breath from her lungs, but she remained cautious. 'Are you inviting a few friends over for the evening?'

'I'm asking you to have dinner with me in town,' he corrected, and now there was almost no doubt in her mind as to what he meant.

'Just the two of us?' she questioned nervously.

'Are you afraid to be alone with me?'

His thumbs were hooked into the broad belt hugging his hips, and his eyes were narrowed and intent upon her face while she tried to imagine what had prompted this invitation after their verbal altercation early that morning.

'Are you afraid?' he repeated his question, intruding on her scattered thoughts.

'No, of course I'm not afraid,' she lied with a glibness that did not usually come easy.

'Well then?'

His eyes mocked and challenged her, and she rose instinctively to meet it. 'I accept your invitation.'

The mockery in his eyes deepened, and she suspected he knew very well that she could have kicked herself at that moment for accepting his challenging invitation to dine with him.

'Be ready at seven,' he ordered, and the next instant she was staring at his broad back as he strode out of her office.

'*Damn!*' Alison muttered to herself when she was alone. It was only now that the full implication of what she had done occurred to her. She had agreed to spend the evening alone in Dirk's company, and it was senseless denying to herself that she was terrified out of her wits at the mere thought. Recalling the accusation he had flung at her that morning made it doubly difficult for her to understand what had prompted him to aproach her with this invitation. Was this perhaps his way of apologising for misconstruing a very innocent gesture?

Alison joined up with the group of tourists and took over from Connie as they walked the short distance down to the cellars, but her mind was not on her job that afternoon. She explained the process of wine-making and answered questions like an automaton, but her thoughts had become centred on the evening that lay ahead of her. At the end of the day she was as nervous and jumpy as a kitten, and a long, relaxing soak in a scented bath did not succeed entirely in dispensing with the nervous tension that was beginning to make her feel as if her insides had become knotted.

She dressed with more care than usual that evening, and selected to wear a cinnamon-coloured silk evening dress which was one of her favourites.

The elbow-length sleeves were wide, and the neckline modest, but the flowing material did not hide the enchanting curve of her breasts and hips, nor the narrowness of her waist. She studied herself in the full-length mirror, her glance sliding critically from her dark brown hair down to the gold sandals on her small feet. The image she projected in the mirror suggested an air of confidence and serenity, but inwardly she was only too aware of a nervous uncertainty that was churning its way through her.

Ferdie wandered into her bedroom while she was sitting in front of the dressing table, and he watched her keenly while she checked her make-up and fastened a small diamond pendant about her throat which had been a gift from one of her foster-parents.

'Where are you going?' asked Ferdie, leaning his elbows on the dressing table and cupping his chin in his hands as he continued to observe her.

'I told you, didn't I, that I'm going out to dinner with your father?'

'Can't I come with you?'

'No, you can't,' she smiled, swinging round on the stool and drawing him towards her so that he leaned against her with his head on her breast. 'You're going to be a good boy and stay here with Salome this evening.'

'Daddy will let me come with you,' he stated confidently. 'I'll ask him when he comes.'

Alison sighed inwardly, but said nothing as Ferdie extricated himself from her arms and bounded out of her room.

Dirk was punctual almost to the second, and when she let him in her heart skipped an uncomfortable beat. He looked magnificent as always in a dark evening suit, and the whiteness of his shirt contrasted heavily with his tanned complexion. She searched his rugged features for some sign of what she could expect that evening, but that mask of cool indifference was firmly in place.

'I want to come with you, Daddy. Please let me come with you!' Ferdie confronted Dirk as he had promised he would.

'You're staying home, and you're going to bed early as usual,' Dirk ordered sternly. 'You've been with me practically all day, and I want to spend this evening alone with your mother.'

'Oh,' said Ferdie, accepting, but not quite understanding what his father had said, and Alison felt like echoing that 'Oh' a little more frantically.

What, exactly, had Dirk meant by that? *I want to spend this evening alone with your mother.* Why should he suddenly want to be alone with her after treating her like a glorified slave these past three months? She was becoming more confused and bewildered with every second that passed, and nervousness seemed to have a stranglehold on her throat when she eventually found herself seated beside Dirk in his Jaguar.

Her hands were locked so tightly together in her lap that she almost had difficulty in unclasping them when they arrived at the hotel in Paarl where Dirk had booked a table for them.

The hotel restaurant was reasonably full, and beyond their table, through the wide arches, a few couples were swaying on the dance floor to the music of the local band. The interior had been designed to encourage relaxation, but Alison was conscious only of the tension aroused by the presence of the man seated opposite her at the small candlelit table. Dirk ordered wine, and from the menu he selected a steak for himself, but Alison chose a small portion of tuna fish and a salad to accommodate her waning appetite that evening.

'You've hardly spoken a word since we left Bordeaux,' Dirk observed with his usual mockery while they drank their wine.

'I haven't been able to think of anything worthwhile to say,' she defended herself stiffly, raising her glass to her lips and taking a sip of wine in the hope that it would steady that awful fluttering in her stomach.

'Why not try relaxing a little?'

'I'm trying to,' she confessed, 'but it isn't easy when I continually find myself wondering why you invited me out to dinner this evening.'

The cold mockery left his eyes, and Alison could almost believe he was smiling at her with genuine amusement. 'Perhaps it's my way of making up for my ungracious behaviour this morning.'

'You mean this is by way of an apology? she said with some surprise, though why she should have felt surprised she could not imagine.

'You could say that, yes.'

'An apology of any kind is quite unnecessary,' she said after a thoughtful pause. 'If our positions had been reversed, then I might have been equally suspicious of your motives.'

The smile in his eyes deepened to a devilish gleam in the candlelight. 'That's very generous of you.'

'Generosity has nothing to do with it,' she retorted stiffly, avoiding his eyes. 'I'm simply being honest.'

Dirk did not reply to that, and they drank their wine in silence for a time until he startled her by saying, 'You look lovely tonight.'

'Thank you,' she managed, her colour deepening when his glance slid over her in a way that made her feel as if he was determinedly probing beneath the silk of her dress. It was silly, she supposed, to feel embarrassed by a man who had known her as intimately as Dirk, but she could not prevent the darkening stain on her cheeks.

'With your hair done up like that you look poised and sophisticated,' he went on, 'but I must admit I prefer it when you leave your hair free of that confining knot.'

Alison overcame her embarrassment, and her confidence was possibly boosted by the wine when she met his gaze levelly. 'If I didn't know you better, I'd say you were flirting with me.'

His eyebrows rose sharply. 'I'm not the only one with a suspicious mind, it seems.'

'That shouldn't surprise you. A few weeks ago you accused me of being suspicious-natured, remember?'

'Are we going to spend the evening sparring with each other across the dinner table?' he asked, his mouth twitching into a semblance of a smile.

'I'm sorry,' she apologised ruefully, remembering what day it was.

'May I fill up your glass?'

She nodded, and when he had done so she raised her glass of wine in a gesture of a salute that drew his attention. 'Happy birthday, Dirk.'

'I was beginning to think you'd never say that,' he mocked her lightly.

'This isn't as good as Bordeaux wine,' she changed the subject after sampling her wine in earnest. 'You're a vintner *par excellence*, Dirk.'

'Who's flirting now?' he mocked her once again, and she stiffened defensively.

'I meant it as a compliment. Your wines are superb.'

'I strive for perfection, but I don't always succeed,' he told her, studying his glass of wine in the glow of the candle as if he were trying to analyse its contents.

'You've always wanted perfection in everything, haven't you? You wanted a perfect wife who would be subordinately docile and absolutely trusting, and when you discovereed that I wasn't quite like that, you shut me out completely.'

She had not intended to say that at all, but she knew it was too late to retract her statement when she saw the smile fade in his eyes to leave them cold and censorious.

'I suggest we change the subject,' he said harshly, and his manner was so forbidding that she slumped back into her former silence.

Their meal was served to them, but Alison's appetite had become almost non-existent. The atmospheric temperature between them felt as if it had dropped several degrees to create that icy barrier she had known so well, and this time she could only blame herself for it.

They both attempted to make polite conversation during the seemingly endless meal, but they failed hopelessly, and when their coffee was served Alison decided to do something about it.

'I'm sorry, Dirk.' She swallowed nervously. 'I shouldn't have accepted your invitation.'

His jaw hardened. 'Why not?'

'This evening has been nothing but a strain on both of us, and I must admit I find it easier hovering in the background with a plate of eats rather than sitting across the table from you.' Humbling herself completely, she added miserably, 'I guess Yvette was right when she said I didn't have potential for very much else.'

Dirk did not comment on this, but his eyes blazed with a sudden fury which she could not understand.

'Dance with me,' he said, getting to his feet and reaching for her hand, and when she tried to tug her hand free, he added softly, 'It's an order.'

With her hand engulfed in the rough warmth of his, she allowed him to draw her to her feet and lead her on to the dance floor, but her heart beat out a rhythm of its own when his arm circled her waist. He held her much too close for comfort, and her steps faltered at the start of the slow waltz when his thighs brushed against her own.

'Dirk . . .'

'Shut up!' he growled close to her ear in such an authoritative voice that she found herself obeying him at once.

The music was dreamy as they moved across the crowded floor, their steps matching perfectly, and as they danced she felt the tension unravelling slowly within her. Dirk, for his size, was surprisingly light on his feet, and for a time she was able to forget everything except the pleasure of dancing with him again for the first time in four years, but her enjoyment soon sharpened into something else when his hand shifted down to the hollow of her back to draw her so close that his chin almost touched her forehead. His nearness had become intoxicating to the point where her blood was beginning to sing through her veins, and his masculine cologne stirred her senses until her pulse quickened to a dangerous pace. Her hand tightened on his shoulder with the intention of pushing him away, but for some inexplicable reason she changed her mind. Her head went down of its own volition until it rested against his broad chest, and for a time she could very nearly make herself believe that nothing had come between them, but the music finally came to a swinging halt, and the dream ended.

Dirk's arm fell away from her with as much reluctance, it seemed, as she raised her head from its comfortable resting place, but when their eyes met, that current of awareness between them deepened to a flow of sensuality so familiar that her breath locked in her throat, robbing her momentarily of speech.

The music started up again, but as Dirk reached for her, she drew away sharply. 'I think it's time we went home.'

CHAPTER EIGHT

IT seemed to Alison as if it took them twice as long to reach the estate, and her nerves were as taut as bowstrings. They travelled the distance in silence; a silence fraught with a tension brought on by that sensual awareness which had flared up between them on the dance floor. Alison felt it not only in herself, but also in Dirk, and she knew it could make the situation twice as difficult for her to cope with. She had never been more vulnerable, and she would have to be on her guard against this storm which was brewing between them.

Alison was inordinately relieved when the Jaguar's piercing headlights swept up Bordeaux's long driveway. Her intention was to escape from Dirk as soon as possible, but her nervousness spiralled into alarm when they stood on her dootstep. Dirk had no intention of leaving her there with a polite 'goodnight', she could see it in the set of his jaw, and in the way he shouldered his way inside and closed the door.

'Thank you, Salome, you may go,' Dirk told the Coloured woman when she put in an appearance and, unaware of the plea in Alison's eyes, Salome bobbed a curtsey and went home.

Alison felt a rising panic at the thought of being alone in the flat with Dirk, and only with a strenuous effort did she manage to appear outwardly calm as she removed her wrap and placed it on a chair with her evening purse. 'I'll make us some coffee.'

'I don't want anything to drink.' Dirk's hand shot out to grip her arm and, without warning, he pulled her roughly into his arms. 'What I want doesn't come in liquid form.'

She had a brief vision of smouldering eyes burning down into hers, but her gasping protest was smothered when his mouth descended on hers with an expertise that parted her lips for an intimate invasion that made her tremble. She had expected some sort of advance, but nothing quite like this. He had acted too swiftly, giving her no time to contemplate defensive tactics, and the feel of his body against her own assaulted her senses with a potency she was incapable of resisting. His hand was in her hair, scattering the pins so that his fingers could move freely through the heavy silken mass, and his arm about her waist was a steel band from which there was no escape as he moulded her softness into the curve of his hard body.

Alison felt as if she were drowning in a sea of her own soaring emotions. His lips left hers to trail a path of sensuous fire down to the base of her throat, and the heat of his hands through the silk of her dress aroused half-forgotten sensations that sent a languorous weakness flowing into her limbs. She knew his need as well as she was beginning to know her own surging desire, but her mind was still clear enough to reject what was happening to her. If she gave in to him now it would be an act of love, but love did not enter into it for Dirk; it never had, and it never would.

'You can't do this to me,' she croaked, her hands thrusting weakly at his shoulders, and her heart pounding so hard and fast that she had found it difficult to speak, but the next instant she felt his fingers tugging at her zip until she felt a cool waft of air against her back.

His warm, moist mouth closed over hers, stifling her protests, but the touch of his strong hands on her supple, responsive flesh was finally her undoing, and she could not suppress the shudder of desire that shook through her when his probing, caressing fingers against her breasts aroused her to the point of pain.

'Don't deny me,' he warned thickly, his warm,

sensual mouth shifting over hers once again, but Alison was no longer capable of denying him anything.

Her body overruled her mind, and her arms were locked about his neck when he lifted her in his arms and carried her the short distance from the lounge into her bedroom. He closed the door with his foot, and when he set her down, she stepped out of her sandals and lowered her arms willingly to let her dress fall down to her feet where it lay unheeded while he removed her lace-trimmed underwear. His touch excited her beyond reason, and his kisses drugged her to the extent that she could not have said how or when he had shed his own clothes, but when he lifted her on to the bed, the touch of his muscled flesh against her own seemed to inflame her.

Dirk's lips and hands roamed her body with a savage intimacy which had once frightened her, but on this occasion she welcomed it. If she could not tell him she loved him, then she could at least show him, and for the first time, her hands caressed him freely, sliding from his wide shoulders down to his slim hips and muscled thighs. She felt him shudder and draw back a little in surprise, then something close to a groan emerged from deep within his throat as he took possession of her. There was no tenderness involved in this fusion of their bodies, only the savagery she had always known, but the years of abstinence had sharpened her desire, and her body responded with a mounting passion that drove the last vestige of coherent thought from her mind. She clung to him ecstatically, her softness yielding to the hard thrust of his body until wave after wave of the most intense pleasure washed over her, and it left her lying next to him, spent and fulfilled, while her head rested on his chest where she could hear his heart thudding as hard and fast as her own.

They did not speak, but she felt that words were unnecessary when their bodies had said so much, and

she did not protest when Dirk left her side moments
later to dress himself. She had slipped into a well of
drowsy content from which she had no wish to
emerge, and, other than pull the bedcover about her,
she did not move, but she followed Dirk's movements
with eyes that did not conceal the strange new
tenderness which spiralled through her.

Dirk shrugged himself into his jacket and pushed
his tie into the pocket as he paused at the foot of her
bed with one hand gripping the post. His eyes met
hers and she was vaguely puzzled by the strange glitter
in their depths. Could it be anger? Surely not! The
words 'I love you' still throbbed in her breast and
hovered unspoken on her lips after the intimacies they
had shared, and it was unthinkable that he had not felt
something close to love for her.

'How many men have there been?'

His abrupt query pierced her dreamy state, and she
shot up in bed, dragging the cover about her naked
body. 'What are you talking about?'

'You know *damn* well what I'm talking about!' the
words spilled harshly from his lips as he leaned
threateningly towards her. 'How many men have you
slept with since you walked out on me nearly four
years ago?'

Alison stared up at him in wild confusion for a
moment, then the colour drained slowly from her face
as understanding dawned and left her speechless with
incredulity that he could have such an abominable
opinion of her.

'Did they pay you well?' he demanded, his eyes
blazing with fury as he supported himself on the bed
with his hands and leaned towards her in such a
menacing manner that she shrank from him in fear and
horror. She wanted to cry out that none of this was true,
that his accusations were unfounded, but the words
seemed to have become locked in her throat as she
watched him straighten and remove his wallet from

the inside pocket of his jacket. 'Well, if you're not going to answer me, then I suppose this will have to suffice.'

He flung a wad of notes on to the bed and, sick with shame and dismay, she stared at it as if it were a viper. He had reduced their lovemaking to something cheap and degrading, and the hurt he inflicted was so intense that it finally brought her out of her frozen stupor.

'*No!*' she cried hoarsely before he reached the door, and when she got off the bed she swept the notes to the floor in one singular movement so that they fluttered like falling leaves on to the carpet. Her eyes were feverishly bright as they met his cold, accusing glance, then something snapped within her and she buried her ashen face in her trembling hands with a rasping, '*Oh, God!*'

'Did you think I wouldn't find out? Did you think I wouldn't guess?' his harsh voice lashed her like the stinging end of a whip. 'God help me, but the way you made love to me tonight was sufficient to make me realise you haven't exactly been living the life of a nun!'

He had misunderstood! She had wanted desperately to show him how much she cared, but all she had succeeded in doing was to make him think her a wanton slut. The pain of this discovery was almost too much to bear, but she managed to calm herself sufficiently to take her robe off the chair beside the bed, and to drape it about her naked, shivering body.

Under Dirk's narrowed, watchful gaze, she picked up the notes she had scattered on the floor and held them out towards him in a hand that shook visibly. In a voice so calm that it was almost lifeless, she said: 'I can understand that you want to punish me for walking out on you and for not telling you about Ferdie, but God knows I don't deserve these insults.'

His jaw hardened, and his cold glance shifted from her white face to the money and back. He had taken his revenge in the cruellest possible way, but he gave no sign of relenting.

'Keep the money!' he barked at her, his gaze sliding over her in a way that made her feel cheap and dirty. 'It was worth every cent!'

Moments later she was alone in her room with the notes still clutched in her hand. She could not control the wave of nausea that rose within her and, flinging the notes on to the dressing table, she dashed into the bathroom to reach the basin with barely a second to spare. The last time she had felt so ill had been when she was in the first stages of pregnancy, but this was a nausea of a different calibre. It left her leaning against the basin, drained and weak, and, for the first time in her life, she wished she were dead. She felt humiliated and beaten, and sick to the very core of her being when the finally dragged herself back to bed. She desperately sought the oblivion of sleep, but it evaded her most of the night, and left her with deep shadows under her eyes the following morning.

She bathed and dressed herself to face the day, and if she tried very hard she might even convince herself that what she had experienced had been nothing but a horrible nightmare, but when she sat down in front of the dressing-table she was confronted by the wad of notes as a hateful reminder of something she would rather have forgotten. He had flung them at her along with those terrible accusations which, even now, made her feel unclean.

Alison felt incapable of coping with anything that morning, and Ferdie, like most children, sensed a certain undercurrent. He was particularly trying at the breakfast table, and she finally resorted to giving him a few hard smacks on the bottom which hurt her more than it apparently hurt him. Afterwards she decided that perhaps she had been at fault, but, whatever the case, the day had started on a singularly unpleasant note.

Dirk had gone to Stellenbosch for the day, so Mike Petzer informed Alison when he had popped into the office briefly that morning, and it was just as well that she did not see Dirk during the day. The humiliation she had suffered at his hands had fast become a simmering anger which helped her to bear the stinging memory of his accusations, but *nothing* could wipe it out altogether.

Ferdie was unnaturally subdued and wary at the dinner table that evening, and that hurt her even more. It was only when she held out her hands to him that he came to her and nestled his head against her shoulder, and tears of remorse filled her eyes when she lifted him on to her lap. She had been partly to blame for the unpleasantness that morning, and it had been unfair of her to smack Ferdie when she had lacked the patience to deal with the situation.

'I'm sorry I was naughty and made you cross, Mummy,' he said in a muffled voice against her shoulder, and her arms tightened about his small frame.

'I was a bit upset this morning,' she murmured, minimising her feelings when, actually, she had been hurting so badly that she had been ready to lash out at anyone and anything. 'Come on, let me put you to bed.'

Ferdie accompanied her without complaining, and the wild frolic they shared before he went to sleep more than made up for everything that had occurred between them that morning, but it did not stop her from feeling ashamed of herself.

Alison felt mentally and physically exhausted after having to endure a sleepless night and a trying day, and she was seriously contemplating an early night when there was a knock on her door. Instinct warned her that it might be Dirk, and she chose to ignore it, but when the knock was repeated, more urgently this time, she decided to answer it for fear of Ferdie being awakened.

Dirk stood on her doorstep, the light from inside illuminating his harsh features, and the mere sight of him made her simmering anger erupt into a roaring flame of furious indignation.

'What do you want?' she demanded, her eyes flashing with the anger she had been forced to keep in check all day.

'I want to talk to you,' he said, forcing his way into her flat and closing the door, and it was anger alone that helped her to sustain his probing glance for several seconds before she turned away from him.

'If it's business, then I have no objections, but, other than that, we have nothing to say to each other.'

'Listen to me.'

No!' she cried, trying to evade the hand that gripped her shoulder.

'Alison!' He swung her round to face him, his hands on her slim shoulders a vice from which she could not escape. 'I owe you an apology.'

'You owe me nothing,' she snapped, her control slipping and angry tears glistening in her eyes. 'You paid for what you got last night, and that was sufficient.'

'Don't say that!' he ordered harshly, his bone-snapping grip on her shoulders almost making her cry out in agony. 'I was wrong about you, and I admit it.'

She blinked back her tears and her usually soft mouth curved in a cynical smile. 'What made you come to that remarkable conclusion?'

'I spent a sleepless night thinking about you.' Dirk released her abruptly and turned from her to walk towards the fireplace with his hands thrust deep into the pockets of his suede pants. 'I came to the conclusion eventually that I'd simply been searching for some way to hurt you, but in the process I hurt myself as well.'

'In your book of laws that makes us quits, I presume.'

Her sarcasm did not escape him, and he turned to

frown down at her. 'Apologising to you doesn't come easy, and you should know that.'

It took a moment for his words to sink in, and her anger petered out as she recognised the truth. She could imagine that it had been a tremendous effort to overcome his stubborn pride sufficiently to enable him to apologise to her, and it would be ungracious of her to reject his magnanimous gesture.

'I accept your apology,' she said at length, much calmer now than she had been before.

'Thank you.'

'There's something you've forgotten,' she stopped him when he would have turned to leave and, unlocking the drawer of the writing desk, took out a bulky envelope and handed it to him with a cool, 'This belongs to you.'

Dirk stared down at the envelope she had placed in his hands and, from the way the muscles stood out along the side of his jaw, she knew that there was no need to enlighten him as to the contents, but his reaction startled her considerably. He flung the envelope, with its contents, on to the glowing coals in the grate, and he stood watching it smoulder for a moment before the flames leapt high in the fireplace. It burned lustily, the paper curling into distorted shapes before it collapsed in ashes, and only then did he turn to look down into her quizzical eyes.

'A man must pay, one way or another, for his stupidity,' he announced grimly, then he strode towards the door and walked out into the night.

Alison stood there for some time staring in stark amazement at the door he had closed behind him, then she turned towards the fireplace where the wad of notes in the grate was now no more than a nondescript pile of white ashes, and somehow it felt to her as if his action had cauterised the wound he had inflicted.

Tears filled her eyes, distorting her vision, and she sat down in a chair in front of the fire and wept until almost every trace of anger and hurt had drained from her.

Alison did not see Dirk again until the Sunday morning. She had dressed comfortably in beige linen slacks, a cotton blouse and sandals, and she was sitting in the lounge helping Ferdie with a jigsaw puzzle when something made her look up. Dirk stood framed in the outer door, and her treacherous pulse quickened at the sight of him, but Ferdie caused a brief diversion as he catapulted towards his father.

'Are you doing anything in particular today?' asked Dirk, lifting Ferdie up into his arms.

Flustered by his presence and that strange glitter in his eyes, Alison steadied her trembling hands by gripping the arms of her chair. 'I haven't anything planned, if that's what you mean.'

'Tell Salome you won't be home for lunch, and come with me.'

It was an order, not a request, and Alison obeyed him instinctively, but when he ushered her towards his white Jaguar parked outside, she paused with uncertainty.

'Dirk, I——'

'Get in, and don't argue,' he instructed, settling Ferdie in the back of the car and giving Alison a gentle push into the front seat.

'Where are we going, Daddy?' Ferdie questioned him as they drove out through the estate gates.

'Yes, Dirk,' Alison echoed Ferdie's query, 'where *are* we going?'

'I thought it would be nice to have a picnic on the banks of the Berg river,' came the unexpected reply, and for a moment she could only think that she was fortunate to be dressed suitably for the occasion.

'A picnic, a picnic, we're going on a picnic!' Ferdie sang excitedly behind them while he held on to the back of Dirk's seat and bounced up and down with glee.

Dirk raised an amused eyebrow and glanced at Alison. 'Does the idea appeal to you as well?'

'Very much,' she confessed. 'I haven't been on a picnic since before . . .'

She had spoken without thinking and she caught her lip nervously between her teeth, but once again Dirk displayed that uncanny habit of reading her thoughts when she would have preferred him not to.

'Since before our marriage?' he finished her sentence for her quizzically, and she clasped her hands tightly in her lap to hide the fact that they were shaking.

'Yes,' she admitted warily, expecting him to mock her in his usual manner, but he did not comment on her remark as he concentrated on his driving, and Alison relaxed sufficiently to let her thoughts wander.

She remembered only too vividly that last picnic on the banks of the river during those weeks before their marriage. It had been a lazy, hot day in mid-January. Ivy Basson had packed them an enormous and inviting picnic lunch, but Alison could not recall that she had eaten very much at all. She had been too aware of Dirk, and that overpowering aura of masculinity which had had her trembling every time he had come near her. Her love for him had been new and fragile, and she had believed, mistakenly, that he had loved her too. Love was not a word that belonged in his vocabulary, and she had been too young and too much in love to notice his lack in expressing his feelings. Desire was the only thing he knew, and he had not changed in that respect.

Bitterness engulfed her like a tidal wave, but she emerged from it swiftly when she realised that they were approaching the picnic site along the banks of the river. This was no time for bitterness when Dirk was obviously making a special effort to be pleasant.

They found a nicely secluded spot and spread out a blanket beneath the shady trees. Dirk opened the boot of the Jaguar and took out a large picnic basket, and then, much to Ferdie's delight, he produced a small cricket bat, a ball, and stumps. Alison made herself comfortable on the blanket while Dirk pushed the stumps into the soft earth and instructed Ferdie in a simplified version of the game of cricket.

Ferdie missed the first few balls, and scowled in a way that sharply resembled Dirk when he was annoyed, but there was cause for great excitement when his bat finally made contact with the ball. The game continued, and Alison was called in later to act as fieldsman. Her attempts to catch the cricket ball were far from professional and totally hilarious from Dirk and Ferdie's point of view, but it created such a warm feeling of unity between them that she found herself relaxing totally.

'You're out, Ferdie!' she cried triumphantly when she succeeded at last in catching the ball in mid-air.

'And so am I,' announced Dirk, wiping the perspiration from his forehead with a handkerchief, and walking into the shade to lower himself on to the blanket.

'I'm hungry,' declared Ferdie, and Dirk groaned in reply.

'Shall I?' asked Alison, gesturing towards the basket, and Dirk nodded.

'Take out whatever there is, and we can help ourselves,' he suggested, stretching his denim-clad figure out on the blanket and leaving her to play hostess.

The basket contained an assortment of sliced cold meat, salads and bread rolls. Dirk eventually opened the bottle of chilled wine while Alison poured fresh orange juice into a glass for Ferdie, and they toasted each other in a teasing manner before they helped themselves to the delicious array of food. The unaccustomed exertion had helped Alison to work up an appetite, and after two glasses of wine she felt pleasantly drowsy. Dirk was lying on his back with an arm flung across his eyes, but Ferdie still had enough energy left to go and play with his new ball and bat. Alison discarded the paper plates and packed everything neatly back into the basket before she, too, followed Dirk's example.

The restful sound of babbling water, and the birdsong in the trees overhead was disturbed only by the distant laughter of others picnicking along the river's edge, and the tranquillity of her surroundings acted like a sleeping draught.

Alison had no idea how long she slept before she became aware of her throat being caressed by someone lying close beside her. She opened her eyes with a start to find Dirk leaning over her, and she would have got to her feet had his hand not gripped her shoulder to hold her pinned to the ground. Her heart was racing much too fast, and her mouth felt dry when she felt his thumb caressing her collarbone at the V-opening of her blouse. His touch was light and sensual, but it was the burning intensity of his eyes that held her captive more than anything else.

'You've lost weight since you came to Bordeaux,' he said quietly, almost as if he was speaking to himself, and her own voice was surprisingly calm when she replied.

'I've been working long hours, as you know very well, and trying to pick up some of the threads of the past hasn't been easy.'

His mouth tightened. 'Do you think these past months have been easy for me?'

'No, I don't suppose they have,' she conceded with honesty after a thoughtful pause.

'I've been doing a lot of thinking since the other night.' Her cheeks flamed, and she looked away, but Dirk caught her chin between his fingers, forcing her to look at him, and what she saw in his eyes made her tremble inwardly. 'Would you be prepared to move in with me and to pick up the threads of your wifely duties?'

Her breath locked in her throat as she stared up at him, and a flood of tenderness engulfed her when she noticed again the sprinkling of grey at his temples. It would be so easy to agree to his suggestion, but she dared not give him a rash answer. Nothing had actually changed, and she was not so sure that she really wanted to pick up where they had left off four years ago.

'I can't answer that now,' she said at length when he began to show signs of impatience. 'I shall need time to think it over.'

'How much time?'

'A few days at least.'

Dirk took his time digesting this, then he nodded slowly and lowered his head until his lips touched the hollow at the base of her throat where her pulse was beating hard and fast. His mouth was warm against her skin as it trailed a slow, sensual path along her throat to that sensitive little spot behind her ear. A shiver of pleasure rippled through her, kindling the fire of her emotions, and when at last his mouth shifted over hers, her lips parted eagerly beneath his. The clean male smell of him stirred her senses, and her hands slid up his arms to become locked in his short, crisp hair. Their kiss deepened, and his mouth moved against hers with a familiar urgency that made the blood skip through her veins. Alison was fast beginning to lose all sense of time and place, but a small voice brought her back to earth with a swift bump.

'What are you doing?' asked Ferdie, sitting on his heels beside them, and observing them with intense curiosity.

'I'm kissing your mother,' Dirk informed him, a wicked gleam in his steel-grey eyes.

'Why?' demanded Ferdie, looking from one to the other.

'Because she blushes so prettily when I kiss her,' Dirk explained, ignoring Alison's efforts to escape the circle of his arms.

'What's "blushes"?' Ferdie continued his questioning, and Alison, red to the roots of her hair, groaned loudly.

'Stop asking so many questions, Ferdie,' she admonished him severely, succeeding at last to push Dirk away from her, and sitting up to straighten her blouse and her hair. 'Isn't it about time we went home?'

Dirk laughed softly, and his laughter was a deep rumble in his throat that was immensely attractive on the ears. He winked conspiratorially at a rather puzzled-looking Ferdie, and together they carried the picnic things back to the car.

The sun was beginning to set when they arrived back at Bordeaux, and this time it was Alison who invited Dirk to stay and share a light meal with them. She was, she admitted to herself, reluctant to let him go while he was in this relaxed mood. He was once again the man she had fallen so madly in love with, and as the evening progressed, she found herself slipping under the spell he was weaving in much the same way as when they had met.

Ferdie's eyelids drooped after dinner, and he was asleep almost the minute Alison put him to bed. He had grown into such a sturdy little boy these past months, and his colour was so healthy that she found it difficult to believe that this was the same fragile child she had had to nurse through so many asthmatic attacks in Cape Town. Her fingers lightly brushed a stray curl away from his forehead, but he did not stir, and a tender smile lurked about her mouth when she switched off the bedside light and went back to the lounge where Dirk was waiting.

'It's been a lovely day,' she sighed happily when he pulled her down on to the sofa beside him, and she was too pleasantly tired to object when he held her in his arms and pushed her head down on to his shoulder.

'I echo that,' he murmured, his fingers sliding through her hair and making her scalp tingle pleasantly.

It felt so perfectly right sitting there like that and, forgetting temporarily the problems which had caused a rift between them, she slipped her arms about his waist and pressed closer to him until the heat of his body warmed her own. She could hear his heartbeats quicken, and he muttered something unintelligible moments before his lips claimed hers in a searing kiss that awakened once again that aching need within her. She felt his fingers tugging at the tiny buttons down the front of her blouse, but in her euphoric state of mind she offered no resistance, and when the front catch of her bra proved to be stubborn, she actually raised her hand beneath his to release the catch.

Her unrequested compliance excited him, she could feel it in the tremor that shook through him, and in his quckened breathing when his hands cupped her breasts. There was no savagery this time as he caressed her and urged her down into a reclining position on the sofa to hold her captive with the hard length of his body, and this strange new gentleness aroused her emotions more sharply than anything had ever done before. Her arms were locked about his neck, her fingers entwined in his hair, and when his lips left hers she could almost believe that it was her own hands that guided his mouth along its fiery path down to her breast.

Alison could no longer think coherently, only feel, and what she felt at that moment was a quickening desire which was like an ache in the lower half of her body. She wanted Dirk at that moment more than she had ever wanted him before, and her breathing was quick and shallow when his sensual tongue lazily circled the hardened peak of her breast. He was exciting her beyond reason, and she was experiencing a pleasure so profound that a low, ecstatic moan escaped her. They were both trapped in the tense grip of desire from which neither of them wanted to escape, but when his impatient fingers tugged at the zip of her slacks, several sharp raps on the front door jarred her mind and her body, and brought a shattering stillness that held her trembling and inert beneath Dirk's equally still frame.

The knock on the door was repeated a little more sharply this time, and only then did they move apart. A muttered curse escaped Dirk, and his eyes were still dark pools of desire while Alison hastily restored a certain amount of order to her clothes. She felt strange, as if everything was happening in slow motion, and her legs were ridiculously unstable beneath her when she finally crossed the room to open the door.

Alison was not sure whom she had expected to find on her doorstep at that time of the evening, but she knew for certain that never in her wildest dreams had she expected to find Yvette Paulson standing there beneath the outside light.

'Where's Dirk?' Yvette demanded without the slightest attempt at politeness and, too numb to speak, Alison opened the door wider so that Yvette could see into the room.

Those large grey eyes shifted beyond Alison, and the hostility which had been there for Alison evaporated instantly at the sight of the man who had risen from the sofa.

'Oh, darling!' Yvette exclaimed, and Alison felt as if she had been turned into stone when that lovely vision of lavender and lace swept past her, and went directly into Dirk's arms like a homing pigeon to its roost. 'I must talk to you Dirk,' Yvette said urgently, clinging to him proprietorially, then she glanced in Alison's direction and added haughtily, 'Privately, if you don't mind.'

Alison stood immobile as the years rolled away until she found herself confronted by a cruel reminder of what had been. With every particle of her mind and heart she willed it to be different on this occasion, but the incident simply followed the same routine. Dirk nodded agreeably and escorted Yvette from the flat, but at the door he paused to face Alison.

'Excuse me,' he said abruptly and in much the same manner as one would excuse oneself from the dinner table, and Alison could not hold back the angry accusation that flashed in her eyes.

Dirk's features settled into that familiar cold mask, shutting her out as he had always done, but this time the pain went far deeper than before, and Alison found herself leaning weakly against the closed door after they had gone.

How could he! How dared he! The words seemed to leap through her mind like an old refrain. How *dared* he make love to her one minute, and calmly walk out the next with Yvette as if she had prior claim to his attentions. How could he do this to her without attempting to offer a reasonable explanation for his behaviour?

Alison drew a sobbing breath as she pushed herself away from the door and she almost ran down the short passage to her room. She flung herself across the bed and wished desperately that she could cry, or scream, or *something*, but the tears would not come, and no sound passed her lips except a low, despairing moan. Her trembling, unfulfilled body was still tingling with the memory of his caresses, yet Yvette simply had to raise her little finger to cool Dirk's ardour and enveigle his attentions, and this was something which Alison found less acceptable now than ever before.

'Would you be prepared to move in with me and pick up the threads of your wifely duties?' Dirk had asked but a few brief hours ago, and she had actually found herself contemplating an affirmative answer, but the answer that raged through her mind at that moment was, '*No! Never!*'

CHAPTER NINE

BORDEAUX had done well on the recent wine show. Three of its white wines were now on the market under the 'Superior' label, and Dirk chose to celebrate this with an elaborate party to which he invited his staff as well as some of his neighbouring friends, and at this function Alison was both hostess and guest. Most of the staff voted for an informal *braai*, and for this purpose tables and chairs were carried out on to the spacious lawn close to the barbeque.

The salads had been prepared by the kitchen staff before they had left to take part in their own celebration that Saturday evening, and that meant that Alison had very little to do except to organise a few willing hands to assist her in carrying everything outside. The fires were lit at five, and shortly afterwards Connie and Myrna arrived with their respective boy-friends. Mike Petzer and his wife, Erica, arrived while the salads were being carried out, and the rest of Dirk's guests arrived in a steady stream during the next half hour until they numbered almost thirty. The atmosphere was jovial, and the wine flowed while the pleasant aroma of meat grilling on the open fires quickened everyone's appetite, but Alison found herself totally incapable of relaxing.

Yvette was there, dressed for the occasion in blue jeans and checked shirt, but even in that casual outfit, she seemed to attract a considerable amount of attention to herself with her slender, often provocative beauty. Her father, Cedric Paulson, accompanied her on this occasion, and Alison could not douse the liking and respect he aroused in her when she found herself in his company for a few brief moments during the course of the evening. Cedric Paulson was as pleasant and harmless as his daughter was nasty and vicious, and Alison found it virtually impossible to understand that these two people could differ so vastly in character.

Alsion stayed out of Dirk's way that evening in much the same way as she had done during the past two weeks since the picnic, but that did not prevent her from being intensely aware of his tall figure towering almost head and shoulders above everyone else. Yvette, however, had no qualms about hovering close to Dirk, and neither did she hesitate to intrude on the *all*-male circle around the fires to cling to Dirk's arm with that sickening familiarity which smacked of possessiveness.

'What that woman needs is a damn good spanking,' Connie murmured when she paused beside Alison and followed the direction of her gaze to where Yvette stood flirting openly with Dirk. 'Just look at the way those men are laughing and lapping up her coquettish behaviour!'

One man was not laughing, however, and that was Cedric Paulson. He looked grim and uncomfortable and, for some inexplicable reason, Alison felt an immense pity well up inside her for this man.

Later in the evening Alison stole away to her flat to make sure that Salome had had something to eat and drink, but when she looked in on Ferdie sleeping so peacefully, she considered it a shame that Salome had to remain there on her own.

'Go off and join your family in this celebration,' she told the Coloured woman, but Salome was hesitant to leave.

'Master Dirk won't like it if *kleinbaas* Ferdie is left alone.'

'Salome,' Alison smiled chidingly, giving her a gentle push towards the door. '*You* know and *I* know that once Ferdie's asleep there's virtually nothing which will awaken him, and he'll be quite safe. I'll lock all the doors, and I'll personally come and check up on him from time to time, so go along and enjoy yourself this evening.'

Alison returned to the party shortly afterwards. She had no appetite whatsoever, but she helped herself to a portion of meat and salads, and sat down next to Erica Petzer to watch a few energetic couples shuffling across the lawn in tune to the music which Dirk had relayed from the house with speakers.

It was a pleasantly warm spring evening, and the sky was clustered with stars after the three days of dismal rain they had had during the week. They could not have chosen a better night to have this *braai*, and everyone appeared to be in a party mood, but for Alison it was fast becoming an agonising ordeal. Dirk was dancing with Yvette, their bodies close, and a provocative smile on Yvette's lips as she looked up into Dirk's face. Alison could perhaps have tolerated the situation if she had not been so aware of the curious glances darting in her direction, and her endurance sank to its lowest ebb when she looked up on one occasion to meet Cedric Paulson's pitying glance.

Humiliation stung her cheeks, and she fled into the house on the pretext of making coffee. She did not pause in her flight until she reached the kitchen, but it was a long time before she could control herself sufficiently to switch on the kettle and make the coffee she had mentioned. Cedric Paulson's pitying glance swam before her pain-filled eyes, and she knew a desire to burst into hysterical tears, but she suppressed it when common sense warned that tears would not solve anything.

Willing hands took the tray of coffee from Alison when she reached the terrace some minutes later, and she hastily returned to the kitchen to collect the tray of snacks she had prepared that afternoon, but her hands had barely gripped the ivory handles when a step behind her made her turn to see Yvette strolling into the kitchen. Her smile was friendly, but the cold, calculating eyes acted as a contradiction.

'I know we've never been friends, and I doubt if we'll ever be friends in the future,' Yvette remarked, casually helping herself to a snack, 'but I feel that I must warn you against reading too much into Dirk's actions.'

Alison had gone rigid at the sight of Yvette, but now it felt as if a rod of cold steel had been inserted into her body to replace her spine. 'I think you should explain yourself.'

'Oh, dear!' sighed Yvette, her voice etched with sarcasm. 'I was hoping I wouldn't have to do that, it's so tiresome, but you obviously need to have everything spelled out for you.'

Alison's blood pressure rose several degrees, but somehow she managed to maintain an outward calmness. 'I'm afraid I've never been good at deciphering veiled insinuations, so I suggest you say exactly what you have to say, and get it over with.'

Yvette helped herself to another snack and took her time as she nibbled at it daintily. It stretched the tension in Alison to breaking point, but she gave no sign of it, and waited in silence until Yvette carefully brushed the crumbs off her fingertips.

'Dirk's attitude towards you has changed lately . . . and don't tell me you haven't been aware of it.'

'I have noticed the change, yes,' Alison admitted, meeting that derisive grey gaze levelly.

'The reason for it is quite simple. He's afraid he might lose Ferdie.'

'Lose Ferdie?' Alison echoed, feeling as if the snow which occasionally capped the mountain peaks in winter had settled on her heart.

'He wants the boy, but he's also very much aware

that the child needs *you*, and that Ferdie will never be
entirely happy on the estate without you, so . . .'

Yvette left her sentence unfinished, but the meaning
was made quite clear to Alison. 'You don't have to say
more.'

'I knew you'd understand eventually.'

'Yes,' Alison snapped, suppressing the desire to slap
that smug look off Yvette's face. 'I *do* understand.'

'Good!' Yvette said abruptly, straightening from her
leaning position against the kitchen table, and, well
aware that she had just delivered a fatal blow, she
adopted an air of childish eagerness which vaguely
bewildered Alison. 'Well, now that I've got that off
my chest, is there perhaps something I could help you
with?'

'There's nothing, thank you,' Alison declined her
offer stiffly. 'I suggest you rejoin the party.'

'See you around, then.'

Yvette sauntered out of the spacious kitchen with all
its modern equipment, but Alison stood there for
several moments like a frozen statue before the pain of
her discovery seared through her like a heated blade.
She wanted to hate Yvette, but she could not. She
had, rather unkindly, been forced to face the reality of
her situation. She ought to be thankful, but her heart
felt like a cold piece of lead in her breast, and it shut
out everything except the bitterness that left the taste
of gall in her mouth.

The dancing was in full swing when Alison finally
emerged from the house. Her movements were
automatic as she deposited a plate of snacks on each
table, and she prayed silently that no one would notice
anything amiss, but when she returned to the kitchen
with the empty tray, she found herself confronted on
the terrace by Mike and Erica Petzer. From the look in
their eyes she knew that they had guessed something
was wrong, but Mike stepped in her path when she
would have turned to flee from them.

'Are you ill, Alison?' he demanded, barring her way to the entrance of the house with its magnificent gables etched against the night sky.

'I'm perfectly well, thank you,' she attempted to assure him, but the light from the entrance hall shone directly into her face, and it told a totally different story which she was incapable of hiding.

Erica moved forward to stand beside her husband. 'Forgive us for interfering, Alison, but you're so pale that you look as if you've seen a ghost.'

'Something has upset me, that's all,' Alison prevaricated, edging towards the door, but Mike barred her way once more, and his lean face was taut with grim determination.

'Substitute "something" for "someone", and I'll take a bet it's Yvette Paulson.'

'Mike!' Erica whispered anxiously, placing a warning hand on his arm as if she thought he had gone too far, but Alison did not hesitate to set his mind at rest.

'It's all right, Erica,' she said, forcing a smile to her frozen lips and turning to face Mike. 'I'd forgotten I'd once confided in you.'

A mixture of triumph and anger sparked in his eyes. 'Then I'm right about a certain lady whose name I shan't mention again.'

'Yes, you're right,' Alison admitted, wincing inwardly as Yvette's tinkling laughter drifted up towards them from the garden.

'What did she do this time?' Mike demanded grimly.

'She took great pains to enlighten me about something, but she actually told me nothing I didn't know already.' Alison's voice was filled with bitterness, and her smile was tight with a cynicism directed at herself. 'It's upsetting to discover that the truth, coming from someone like her, has a way of hitting hard where it hurts most.'

Mike's glance sharpened. 'You're not thinking of leaving again, are you?'

The thought had not yet occurred to her, but now she found herself admitting, 'I might have to.'

'But why?'

'The situation here has become intolerable for me, and I refuse to live the rest of my life in the shadow of another woman,' Alison confessed, the words torn from her as if by some force which she could not control.

'What do you mean?' Erica intervened again, her eyes bewildered and questioning as her glance darted from Alison to Mike.

'I'll explain later,' Mike hastily brushed aside her query, then he focused his attention on Alison, and this time there was a definite note of pleading in his voice. 'Don't make any hasty decisions, Alison. It would break everyone's spirit here on Bordeaux if we have to go through another period like the one after you walked out on Dirk.'

'Aren't you being a bit melodramatic, Mike?' Alison laughed mirthlessly. 'The well-being of the staff here on Bordeaux surely doesn't depend on my coming or going?'

'You'd be surprised.' His hand gripped her shoulder as if to stress what he was saying. 'During these few short months you've become an essential part of the proceedings here on the estate. Bordeaux's Coloured community has a great liking and respect for you, and they all remember only too vividly what Dirk had been like after you had left.'

The devil was rampant here on Bordeaux, Salome's words returned unbidden to Alison's mind, and she felt herself squirming inwardly like a fish caught on a baited hook.

'You're making it very difficult for me, but I imagine you know that,' she remarked with a cold anger born of sheer desperation.

'You have the right to make your own decisions,' Mike conceded, his hand falling away from her shoulder. 'I'm simply pointing out certain factors which I feel need your earnest consideration before you decide one way or the other.'

To Alison it felt as if he had thrown a boulder in her path. She knew he had meant well, and that he was thinking, not only of her, but of everyone else on the estate, but at that precise moment she could not conjure up an appreciation for his sound logic. She could think only of herself, and the trap which had sprung so successfully to keep her a prisoner on Bordeaux soil. From the recesses of her memory came the remembered vision of an impala ram caught in the vice-like jaws of an illegal trap, and she experienced at that moment the pain and anger of that thrashing animal.

'Thanks!' she snapped, directing her icy anger at an undeserving Mike. 'Thanks for nothing!'

She pushed past him and went into the house where she had been mistress for such a brief spell in her married life. She walked blindly, her footsteps muted by the thick pile of the carpet, but she was shaking uncontrollably when she reached the sanctuary of the empty kitchen. The tray slipped from her nerveless fingers, but she caught it smartly and placed it on the table, and then, to her horror, she burst into tears.

Unable to control herself, and afraid that someone might find her there in that tearful state, she escaped through the kitchen door and almost ran the short distance to her flat. There, in the privacy of her bedroom, choking sobs tore through her slim body, and several minutes elapsed before she finally regained control of herself. She sponged her face with cold water and repaired the damage to her make-up with a concerted effort to hide all traces of her despicable bout of weakness. Only when she was wholly satisfied with her appearance did she leave her flat to return to the party, and as the evening wore on she found sufficient courage from somewhere to face everyone with a smile that successfully hid the misery in her soul.

Towards midnight Dirk asked Alison to dance with him, and, for the sake of propriety, she could not refuse. His arm was firm about her waist, and when their bodies touched she felt the ice melting in her veins, but not even the sweet agony of his nearness could eliminate entirely the coldness wrapped about her heart.

'You've been avoiding me all evening,' he accused as they swayed slowly in time to the music. 'Now that I come to think of it, you've been avoiding me these past two weeks.'

'I've been busy.'

'That's the excuse you've used every time I've wanted to spend an evening in your company,' Dirk mocked her. 'Don't you think it's becoming a bit worn?'

His accusation was exactly the antidote she had needed to overcome her physical awareness of him, and the spurt of anger that erupted within her helped to strengthen her considerably.

'Are you accusing me of lying about the amount of work I've had to wade through before this evening?'

'I wouldn't exactly accuse you of lying, but I firmly believe you've been fabricating excuses not to see me,' he persisted in that same mocking manner.

'You told me when I came here that my evenings were my own to do with as I pleased unless you required my services, and if I chose to spend my evenings going over the preparations for this evening, then I was quite at liberty to do so,' Alison argued defensively, and when she happened to look up at him she saw a look of annoyance flash across his harsh face.

'Dammit, Alison!' he growled softly close to her ear. 'After the Sunday we picnicked together I thought we'd reached a certain amicable stage in our relationship.'

'After that Sunday I've been made to realise that nothing has really changed,' she corrected him coldly. 'Those barriers we erected between us so long ago are still there, and instead of crumbling, they've become much stronger.'

'You don't know what——'

'Dirk?' a familiar honeyed voice interrupted his forceful reply and forced them to halt in the middle of the waltz. 'You promised me the last dance, remember?'

It seemed for a moment as if Dirk was going to contradict that statement, then he changed his mind, and his face was an inscrutable mask when he said smoothly, 'So I did.'

'See what I mean?' Alison smiled cynically up into his narrowed eyes when his arms fell away from her, and she did not wait to watch him take Yvette into his arms before she turned away and walked out of the party to return to the silence and solitude of her flat.

She went to bed, but she could not sleep. Her mind was in a frantic turmoil from which only two statements, made to her that evening, stood out clearly. The one had come from Yvette: 'He wants the boy, but he's also aware that the child needs you and that he'll never be entirely happy without you.' And the other came from Mike: 'It would break everyone's spirit here on Bordeaux if we have to go through another period like the one after you walked out on Dirk.'

These two statements, disorientated as they might seem, had great bearing on each other. The one produced an instinctive desire to cut her losses and run, while the other bound her more securely to her uncertain moorings. Her mind, like a see-saw, flipped from one to the other, and it was only when she reached a point of sheer exhaustion that she allowed herself to face the obvious answer to her problem. To run would be an act of cowardice, to stay would take great courage, and courage was something Alison had never lacked. Four years ago she had been confused and unhappy, and she had carried within her the child of a man who had callously delivered her with an ultimatum when all she had wanted was to understand the reason for the intimacy she had so often witnessed between him and Yvette. 'If you leave now don't think you can ever come back,' Dirk had said and, stripped temporarily of her courage, she had fled like a coward. But not this time—*not this time!*

Alison eventually went to sleep with her mind firmly settled on that thought, but she had no way of knowing how soon her courage would be put to the test.

It was raining the Sunday morning when Alison awoke, and she found it almost impossible to believe when she thought of the cloudless, starry sky the night before. There had been no warning of more rain to come, but now, as she looked up at the sky from her bedroom window, it was completely shrouded in a blanket of grey clouds.

Ferdie, like most children, was particularly trouble-some at having to remain indoors. The rain was as fine as a sheet of mist, but as dampening as a downpour, and she could not risk him becoming ill. Out of pique, more than anything else, Ferdie went to sleep after lunch, and Alison was contemplating something of a similar nature when the summons came via Salome that Dirk wanted to see her privately in his study.

A summons from Dirk was not something one ignored, and Alison, irritated as she was at that moment, could not ignore it.

Dirk was standing in front of the window when she entered his study, but he was standing with his back turned towards her, and he was seemingly unaware of her presence until she knocked lightly on the door to draw his attention. He turned then, and his eyes narrowed instantly at the sight of her, but Alison, in turn, was observing him cautiously. Dressed in black pants and black open-necked shirt, he looked like the devil himself, and a grey snakeskin belt was the only item of clothing to relieve the sombreness of his attire. He gestured that she could come inside and close the door, and she did so with a measure of alarm at being closeted in the same room with this dark devil who was observing her with such intensely cold eyes.

'You certainly took your time in getting here,' he accused unfairly, and it was only with the greatest difficulty that Alison clamped down on the anger that rose so swiftly within her.

'I came as soon as I received your message that you wanted to see me.'

His dark brows drew together in a straight line of obvious annoyance as he lessened the distance between them to tower over her in a way that she felt instinctively was menacing. She felt the muscles in her legs bunch together in preparation for a hasty retreat, but somehow she managed to remain standing where she was.

'I asked you a question two Sundays ago, and I think it's time you gave me an answer,' he barked at her, behaving as if the conversation between them the previous evening had not occurred, and after a startled pause she decided to follow suit.

'Yes, I suppose I do owe you an answer,' she replied with a vagueness which deserved to be complimented.

'Well?'

'My answer is "no",' she replied calmly, and Dirk's jaw hardened.

'May I know why?'

'I have no intention of walking back into the same situation I walked out on years ago,' she retorted hotly, his autocratic manner finally succeeding in arousing her anger. 'I refuse to be used, Dirk. Not for Ferdie's sake, or anyone else's.'

'Ferdie?' he echoed with a bewildered look on his face which might have fooled her if she had not been so painfully aware of the truth.

'Yes, Ferdie!' she repeated sharply, her eyes flashing with anger. 'You're afraid to lose him. You know he needs me as much as he needs you, so you decided it would be a great idea if we got together again.' She paused only briefly to laugh cynically up into his granite hard features before she continued. 'Oh, your motive is commendable, but what you're really afraid of is that I might walk out and take Ferdie with me.'

A deathly silence followed her outburst, then his wrath erupted about her with a violence that made her shudder and take an involuntary pace backwards. 'Ferdie will stay here where he belongs, and I'll be father and mother to him if I have to, but I don't give a damn whether you go or stay!'

Having the truth thrust home to her the previous evening had been painful enough, but, coming from Dirk, it was unbearable, and the blood drained from her face to leave her deathly white: 'So Yvette was right after all.'

'What does Yvette have to do with this discussion of ours?' he demanded with a savage snarl, and only then did Alison realise that she had spoken her thoughts aloud.

'Yvette has everything to do with it,' she replied in a voice that sounded flat and unlike her own. 'Last night she pointed out a few things to me that I'd already known, but had conveniently brushed aside, and she took a great delight in stressing the fact that the only reason you wanted to resume our marriage was because of Ferdie.'

That familiar mask shifted into place, hiding his true feelings from her as he said with infuriating calmness, 'I see.'

'I'm glad you do, and I appreciate it that you're not attempting to deny her allegations by lying to me,' she confronted him with the truth as she saw it. 'You don't care about me, and you never have. When I walked out on you four years ago your pride was the only thing which suffered a dent, but now there's Ferdie, and as you said a moment ago, you don't give a damn whether I go or stay. And that, Dirk, is proof enough for me of how much you really care.'

'Alison!' he thundered protestingly, white about the mouth as he reached for her, but she was blind to everything except her own pain.

'Don't touch me!' she cried sharply, backing away from him towards the door. 'And don't come near me *ever* again!'

He gestured impatiently, but kept his distance. 'Listen to me for a moment!'

'No, *you* listen to *me*, Dirk du Bois!' she spat out the words, and all the bitterness and misery of the past years was in her ragged voice and in the grey-green eyes that blazed up at him from her white face. 'I've taken about as much from you as any human being can stand, and if you think I'm going to walk out and leave Ferdie here alone with you, then you can think again. I'll be your slave, and I'll work my fingers to the bone for you, if that's what you really want, but don't *ever* again expect more from me than you would from any other employee on this estate.'

'Alison——'

'I hate you, do you hear me, Dirk! *I hate you!*' she cried with an unnatural vehemence, then she wrenched open the door and fled, her breath coming in choking sobs as she ran the distance back to her flat, but when she stood panting in the centre of her lounge she knew that she could not sit there calmly after what had occurred.

The keys to her car lay on her writing desk, and she snatched them up in passing as she ran out to her car and flung herself into the driver's seat. She had to get away somewhere by herself; she had to think, and she could not do so here on Bordeaux where everything seemed to be closing in on her. The past and the present had come together with torturous effects, and she could not bear the agony of it.

The Renault, sluggish at first, picked up speed and shot past the main house. The drive down to the arched entrance seemed endless, and Alison could not shrug off that horrible feeling that at any moment someone might rush out at her to prevent her from leaving, but nothing happened, and a sigh of intense relief escaped her when she finally turned on to the main road leading to Stellenbosch. She had no particular reason for driving towards Stellenbosch, and neither did she have any fixed idea in her mind where she was going. All she wanted was to get away on her own for a while, and driving somehow helped to rationalise her thoughts while her mind processed the indescribable pain which was such a throbbing, living thing inside of her.

There was a lull in the rain, but the tyres still hissed on the wet tarmac, and passing vehicles threw up a spray which necessitated the use of windscreen wipers. There were not too many cars on the road, and Alison's foot went down on the accelerator, an action to which the small car responded with a burst of speed. The countryside was green and lush after the recent rains, and wherever one looked the vineyards were sprouting a strong new growth, but Alison saw none of this. She saw only Dirk's harsh face and those cold, indifferent eyes as he stated savagely, 'Ferdie will stay here where he belongs, and I'll be father and mother to him if I have to, but I don't give a damn whether you go or stay!'

I don't give a damn whether you go or stay. That summed up the situation exactly. Go or stay . . . go or stay . . .! The words reverberated through her tortured mind, but she had made her decision. She would *stay*. It was going to be hell on earth, but she was not going to walk out again. She would stay for Ferdie's sake; for *everyone's* sake, and perhaps ... perhaps, in the far distant future, fate might be kinder.

Her thoughts were miles away when a black, mangy dog darted across the road directly in front of her car, and she reacted instinctively. Her foot went down on the brake and she swerved sharply to avoid the animal, but even as she did so, she felt the wheels of the car skidding on the wet tarmac. The dog darted, unharmed, down the embankment and through the fence, but Alison was losing her battle to regain control of her car. She had a weird feeling that everything was happening in slow motion, but at that moment there was no fear attached to the incident. The Renault slid towards the edge of the road and seemed to hover there for endless seconds before it rolled down the slanted embankment.

The world spun crazily to the accompanying sound of crunching metal and shattering glass, and then, miraculously, the Renault was swaying on its wheels again. Alison sat there for a few stunned seconds. Bits of glass lay everywhere, and she was amazed that she was still in one piece, but moments later she was vaulted into action at the sight of flames darting from beneath the bonnet. She tried both doors, but they were jammed, and it was only then that she realised she had strapped herself in without actually being aware of it. She tugged at the release catch of the seat-belt, but it obstinately refused to budge, and her hands were shaking so much that she could not rectify the fault. The flames were leaping higher from beneath the bonnet, and fear was beginning to take a hold on her as she felt the heat against her face through the shattered windscreen.

Alison tugged frantically at the seat-belt, her fingers futilely depressing the faulty release catch. If she could release the catch then she might stand a chance of escaping through the broken window beside her, but the belt remained firmly in place, and the heat of the flames was fast becoming unbearable.

'Here, let me help you,' someone said beside her, and she looked up into the face of a strange young man in a red leather jacket. She was too choked with fear to speak as he produced a knife and released the lethal-looking blade with a flick of his thumb. He deftly slit the seat belt to release her, and moments later she was being lifted through the window to safety. 'Is there anyone else in there?'

'No,' she answered his query in a choked voice.

'Look out!' he shouted the next instant and, simultaneously, she was flung down on to the ground against the side of the embankment. A deafening explosion made the damp earth shudder beneath her, and the acrid smell of burning petrol and rubber was in her nostrils when she finally raised her head to look over her shoulder. The Renault was being engulfed in what seemed like a ball of smoke and fire, and only then did the horror of what might have happened thrust its way home to her. She was shaking like a leaf and sobbing without actual tears coming to her eyes, and it was at that moment that she became aware once again of the fair-haired young man lying there on the embankment beside her. He sat up and studied her intently. 'Are you hurt anywhere?'

'No, I—I don't think so,' she stammered, making an effort to pull herself together, and mentally checking whether she could detect any sign of pain anywhere in her body.

'You've had a very lucky escape, do you know that?'

'Yes,' she swallowed convulsively. 'And I have you to thank for it.'

She followed his glance in the direction of her now smouldering car, and found herself silently echoing his remark. She had been very lucky; *very* lucky indeed.

'I'm afraid your car is beyond repair,' he observed in a manner which made it seem as if the thought pained him as much as it did her.

'I'm afraid so,' she replied dismally, aware suddenly of strange voices coming from above them and, when she looked up, she realised that several cars had stopped to witness the incident. Anxious now to get away, she allowed her rescuer to pull her to her feet, and his hand remained firmly beneath her elbow as he helped her up the embankment and on to the road while the inquisitive onlookers continued to stare. 'Do you think you could give me a lift to the Solitaire estate?' she asked when she suddenly realised that they were actually standing less than a stone's throw away from Solitaire's vineyards. 'I have friends there,' she added persuasively.

The young man nodded and led her away from the small crowd of people who were beginning to fire questions at them, and moments later she was thankful that she was wearing slacks when she discovered that her rescuer's means of conveyance was a powerful-looking motorcycle.

'You've never ridden one of these, have you?' he grinned, interpreting her dubious expression correctly.

'Never,' she confessed, and he was very helpful after that. He fastened the spare safety helmet beneath her chin, told her where to put her feet and, for the rest, she simply had to cling to him for dear life.

'Solitaire estate, you say?' he asked, glancing at her over his shoulder as he kicked the engine to life.

'Yes,' she shouted back above the roar. 'It's less than a kilometre from here.'

The next instant she was clutching wildly at his leather jacket as they sped away from the scene of the accident which could so easily have ended fatally for her.

CHAPTER TEN

SOLITAIRE's Gothic gables became visible among the trees, and to Alison it had never been a more welcome sight. She was beginning to feel the after-effects of the experience she had lived through, and her insides were shaking like jelly. She felt slightly bruised across her shoulder and her midriff where the seat-belt had bitten into her, and her forehead was stinging as if from a cut.

The roar of the motorcycle must have drawn Kate's attention, for the heavy oak door was flung open before they had had time to knock, and one look at Alison's dishevelled appearance was enough to make her pale visibly.

'Alison!' she exclaimed, rushing forward without hesitation. 'For God's sake, what happened?'

Her glance went from Alison to the young man standing beside her, but it was Alison who replied unsteadily. 'I had an accident with my car about a kilometre from here, and this young man very kindly gave me a lift to your doorstep.'

Kate assimilated the shock of this information swiftly, then she gestured with her hands. 'Come in, both of you.'

'I'm afraid I'm on my way to meet my girl-friend in Stellenbosch, and I'm running a little late for our date as it is,' Alison's rescuer declined hastily, then he raised his hand in a vague salute. 'Glad to have been of service.'

Alison tried to stop him, but he was down the steps and riding away on his motorcycle before she could do anything about it. 'Oh, dear, I—I didn't even ask his name.'

'Never mind that now,' Kate murmured comfortingly, placing an arm about Alison's shoulders. 'Come in and sit down.'

Alison could not think coherently at that moment, and she was only too happy to let someone else take over, especially someone as competent and efficient as Kate. She was taken through to the bathroom, and there Kate helped her to clean herself up a little. She felt considerably better when the dirt was removed from her face and hands, but Kate had not finished with her yet. The first-aid box was hauled out, and, in silence, Kate disinfected the slight cut close to the hairline which Alison had now become more aware of. A narrow strip of Elastoplast was placed over it deftly, and only then did Kate lead Alison into the living-room with its familiar beams against the ceiling and antique furnishings.

A tray of tea seemed to appear magically as Alison lowered herself rather gingerly into a comfortable chair, and Kate poured out a strong cup for both of them.

'Just what the doctor ordered,' she smiled briefly as she handed Alison hers. 'Drink that up, then you can tell me all about it.'

Alison obeyed in silence, and drank her tea under Kate's watchful eyes. She was still shaking, she could feel the tremors of shock cascading throughout her body, and she realised, not for the first time, how fragile the thread between life and death. She had strapped herself into the seat of her car without actually realising it. It had been an act of sheer habit, but it was a habit which, she knew now, had almost certainly saved her life. She could have been dead; at this moment she could have been lying cold and lifeless along the side of the road, or in her mangled car. What happened afterwards did not bear thinking about, for the mere thought of it made her shudder.

'There isn't much to tell,' she said in a flat,

unfamiliar voice when Kate had removed the empty tea-cup from her trembling hands. 'It was really all my own fault. I was travelling too fast on the wet road when a dog darted across in front of me. I tried to avoid it, and my car went into a skid. It left the road, and rolled down the embankment.'

Putting it into words made her live through those terrifying moments mentally, and she shuddered once again as she felt the heat of those flames against her face.

'You're lucky to be alive,' Kate voiced the words which circled repeatedly through Alison's mind.

'I wouldn't have been so lucky if I hadn't been wearing my seat-belt, but the belt also became a hazard in the end.' She had a mental vision once again of flames darting from beneath the bonnet of her car, and she felt again the heat against her unprotected face. She felt her fear too, and instantly shut her mind to it as she continued speaking. 'The car had caught alight, and I was shaking so much that I couldn't undo the belt which had somehow jammed in the accident. If the gentleman who brought me here hadn't come along at just the right time to help me out, then I——'

She paused abruptly, unable to continue, and Kate said incredulously. 'Don't tell me your car burnt out.'

Alison nodded and swallowed convulsively. 'It exploded mere seconds after I was pulled clear of the wreckage.'

The full horror of what had happened was upon Alison, and neither was Kate unaffected by what Alison had told her. Her face had gone so white that her eyes had become the only visible splash of colour.

'Oh, my God!' Kate breathed out the words huskily, then she leapt to her feet. 'I'd better let Dirk know you're here, and you're safe.'

'Please don't,' Alison stopped her at once, gesturing nervously. 'Not yet, anyway.'

Kate looked puzzled as she lowered herself into the

chair facing Alison. 'Dirk will be concerned when he finds out that you haven't reached your destination.'

Alison shook her head miserably and stared down at her hands which she clasped so tightly in her lap. 'I wasn't going anywhere in particular, and besides, I—I don't think he even knows I've left the estate ... or cares, for that matter.'

'Alison?' Kate leaned forward to touch her arm, and that dreadful calmness seemed to snap inside Alison.

'Oh, Kate, I—I've been unhappy before, but this time...' Alison paused to draw a ragged, steadying breath, then she added dully, 'If it wasn't for Ferdie I could almost wish that I'd died in those flames.'

'Don't say that!' Kate rebuked her sharply.

'What else is there to live for except Ferdie?' Alison argued quietly. 'Dirk doesn't care ... he told me so.'

'And you still care about him?'

'I'm afraid I've never stopped loving him,' Alison confessed, and her mind darted back to the conversation she had had with Dirk earlier that afternoon. 'When I confronted him with the fact that he was afraid I might take Ferdie and walk out, he said Ferdie's place was on Bordeaux, but he didn't give a damn whether I went or stayed.'

An almost physical pain seared through her as she spoke those words, and it was there in the eyes she raised to Kate's.

'Hello, what's going on here?' Rhyno's voice interrupted the ensuing silence, and they both looked up at the tall, lean man who had come into the living-room.

'Alison has had an accident with her car,' Kate told him quietly, and an expression of shock replaced the faint smile on his tanned features.

'Don't tell me it was *your* car I saw smouldering about a kilometre from here?' he questioned Alison.

'Yes,' Alison managed thickly.

'Darling, I want you to stay here with Alison,' Kate intervened swiftly before Rhyno could say any more, then her glance shifted back to Alison. 'I think it's time I telephoned Dirk.'

Alison shrank from the idea, but she nodded agreeably, and moments later she was alone in the living-room with Rhyno.

'What happened?' he asked, lowering his lean length into the chair Kate had vacated, and Alison briefly went over the frightening incidents which had led up to her arrival on Solitaire. When her voice finally faltered to a stop she found Rhyno's dark eyes studying her intently. 'I think I should get the doctor out to take a look at you. You could be suffering from concussion, or any number of things.'

'That won't be necessary, thank you, Rhyno,' she contradicted hastily. 'I feel a bit bruised and shaken, but otherwise I'm fine.'

Rhyno did not press the matter, and a few moments later Kate returned to the living-room with the most peculiar expression on her lovely face. It was a mixture of nervous excitement and triumph, and Alison found it totally confusing.

'I've spoken to Dirk, and he's coming over right away,' she said, seating herself on the arm of Rhyno's chair and draping an arm about his shoulders as she added severely, 'Darling, I want you to make yourself scarce when Dirk arrives, and leave the rest to me.'

Rhyno raised his dark gaze to his wife's, and what he saw there made him ask sternly, 'What devious plan are you hatching, Kate?'

'The truth is, I wasn't hatching any sort of plan until I spoke to Dirk, but——' she paused and smiled with that same mixture of excitement and triumph.

'What did he say?' asked Alison in a stilted voice.

'Not very much, I'm afraid,' Kate replied with a shrug, then she added in a more serious vein, 'He thinks you're dead.'

'Oh, no!' Alison gasped in something akin to horror, and raised a trembling hand to her tight throat.

'For God's sake, Kate, what did you tell the man?' Rhyno exploded with an anger that made Alison flinch, but Kate seemed to take her husband's outburst in her stride.

'Nothing much,' came the innocent but uninformative reply.

'But you must have said *something* to make him think Alison is—is dead?' Rhyno insisted sharply, stumbling uncharacteristically over his words in his frustration and anger.

'I told him Alison had been involved in an accident, and that her car had caught alight after it had rolled down the embankment,' Kate explained calmly. 'Before I could reassure him of her safety he was thundering away at me without giving me a further opportunity to explain.'

'What did he say?' Alison asked again, this time more faintly.

'He demanded to know where you were, and naturally I told him you were here,' Kate continued in that serene manner which Alison now realised hid an inner excitement. 'It was only when he insisted that you shouldn't be removed from here before he's had a chance to see you that I began to realise he thought you'd died in the accident.'

'And you left him to think the worst?' Rhyno stormed at her with an incredulous anger.

'I couldn't very well tell him more when he'd slammed the phone down in my ear, now could I?' Kate argued testily, her glance shifting from Rhyno to Alison and back.

'Kate!' Rhyno sighed exasperatedly, a faint glimmer of a smile making its hesitant appearance about his strong mouth. 'The things you do make my hair stand on end at times!'

'It won't do the brute any harm to stew in his own juice for a while,' Kate retorted with conviction. 'And it's one way for Alison to find out exactly how much he cares for her.'

'You're playing a dangerous game,' Rhyno warned, while Alison felt compassion for Dirk struggling to the forefront of her chaotic mind.

'It's a game Dirk started by jumping to the wrong conclusion, and not even he can deny that,' the slender, silvery-haired woman seated on the arm of Rhyno's chair announced firmly.

Afraid suddenly, Alison shifted her weight to the edge of her chair. 'Kate, I . . .'

'Relax, Alison,' Kate interrupted her. 'Fate has taken a hand, and if I'm not mistaken, you're going to know the truth soon enough.'

The truth, Alison thought cynically. She knew the truth already. What Kate was hoping for was totally impossible, and the only reaction they would receive from Dirk would be that savage anger that made her shrivel inwardly at the mere thought of it.

'I'll be in the study if you should need me,' Rhyno announced as he got to his feet, but when he would have passed Kate she caught at his hand and curled her fingers about his.

'Thank you, Rhyno.'

'I think you're crazy,' he announced grimly, then he smiled unexpectedly and lowered his dark head to kiss her lightly on the lips. 'But I still love you.'

He walked out then, leaving Kate and Alison alone in the living-room, and they sat facing each other in silence for a moment before Kate smiled encouragingly and said: 'All we have to do now is wait.'

Wait. Wait for what? Alison wondered miserably, but she did not have the heart to burst Kate's bubble of excitement.

It had started raining again, a fine shower that misted up the windows, and Alison was beginning to feel as dismal as it looked outside. She was nervous and tense, and she was still considerably shaky after what she had been through, but Kate kept the conversation going while they sat there waiting. The tea was still warm in the pot, and she poured out a second cup for both of them, but Alison could barely swallow hers down. Her throat felt too tight, and her anxiety grew with every tick of the clock on the mantelshelf. She tried to work out how long it would take Dirk to travel from Bordeaux to Solitaire, but her mind refused to function in a mathematical direction.

Kate did most of the talking during that long, nerve-racking wait, and Alison answered her automatically, scarcely knowing what she was saying. All she could think of was Dirk, and all she could see was that savage glint in his eyes. *I don't give a damn!* Oh, God! she groaned inwardly. None of this could possibly change his feelings. He didn't give a damn, and that was that!

The sound of a car coming up the drive brought Kate to her feet, and it filled Alison with something close to terror.

'That must be Dirk,' said Kate, walking across to the window to look outside. 'Yes, it is him.'

'Kate!'

Alison had leapt to her feet in alarm, but Kate's hands were instantly on her shoulders, and she was pushed unceremoniously back into her chair. 'Sit down and, whatever you do, stay calm.'

Calm? She felt like laughing hysterically at the word. Would she ever feel quite calm again?

Her frightened eyes followed Kate's tall, slim figure as she walked out of the living-room and left the door slightly ajar so that Alison could hear but could not see what was going on in the spacious entrance hall beyond.

'Where is she?' Dirk's deep, booming voice demanded moments later, and the mere sound of it made Alison's nerve-ends quiver frantically as she stared panic-stricken at the door.

'In there,' Kate's voice replied levelly.

Heavy footsteps approached the living-room and, quite suddenly, Alison felt a strange, almost unnatural calmness shifting over her. Her rigid back relaxed, and her ragged breathing became more regular with every sound of his step on the polished wooden floor. The door was pushed open, and then Dirk stood framed in it. Or *was* it Dirk? she found herself wondering crazily.

His pallor was a sickly grey against the blackness of his shirt, and his hair hung damply, and untidily across his broad forehead as if his fingers had combed through it agitatedly more than once. The eyes that burned into hers across the distance that separated them were wild with an unmistakable anguish, and they reached out somehow to the very core of her being.

'Alison!' her name passed his lips in a hoarse, unfamiliar voice, and then, somehow, he was kneeling in front of her, his hands shaking visibly as they slid over her in a way that seemed to convey that he was trying to convince himself that she was alive, while at the same time searching for possible injuries. 'Are you hurt?'

'A bit bruised and—and shaken, but not—not hurt,' she managed in a whisper, unable to take her eyes off this white-faced man at her feet who was so familiar and yet so strange at that moment.

'Are you sure?'

'I'm sure.'

He lightly fingered the small strip of Elastoplast against her forehead, and then those wild eyes were burning into hers again. 'Did you—were you——'

'Trying to kill myself?' she filled in for him when he seemed to falter, and when he nodded she said: 'No, I wasn't.'

The look of relief that shifted over his face filled her with an aching tenderness, but she suppressed the desire to draw his head down against her breast in much the same way as she did with Ferdie when he needed to be comforted. Her action might be misconstrued, and she could not bear his mockery at that moment.

'Alison . . .' Dirk's hands found hers and gripped them tightly, but it was that unfamiliar pleading in his faintly bloodshot eyes that held her captive. 'Come home with me?'

Never before had she seen him so stripped of his arrogant, confident manner, and it hurt to see him like that. It hurt to see this proud man humbled and kneeling at her feet. There was a time when she might have wanted to see him like that, but not now, and not ever again.

'I'll come home with you,' she said in a choked voice, and once again that look of relief washed over his pale, haggard features.

He drew her to her feet and placed a hand beneath her elbow as they walked out of the living-room, but other than that he did not attempt to touch her.

Kate had remained discreetly out of the way, but when they encountered her in the hall, Dirk placed his hand on Kate's shoulder and said roughly, 'Thanks for your help.'

'It was my pleasure,' announced Kate, darting a glance at Alison, but the query in her eyes was one which Alison could not answer as yet.

Dirk and Alison drove back to Bordeaux in silence, and when they passed the wreck of her car his only reaction was a tightening of his hands on the steering wheel of the Jaguar. His strong profile looked grim, but his colour had improved to some extent, and Alison could not help wondering what he was thinking while she sat there quiet and tense beside him.

Was she simply imagining something which was not there? Could she interpret the way he had behaved to mean that he did care for her after all? It could surely not have meant anything else, could it?

Yvette's red Triumph was parked in the driveway of his home when they arrived at Bordeaux, and Alison felt her hopes shrivel up and disintegrate into ashes. She glanced searchingly at Dirk, but his expression gave nothing away as he parked the Jaguar close to the steps and helped her out. They walked into the house in silence, but Yvette rose from a chair when they entered the living-room, and she flew across the room to throw herself at Dirk in characteristic fashion.

'Darling, I've been waiting simply ages! Where have you been?' Over Dirk's shoulder she saw Alison observing them in silence, and her joyful expression altered at once to pure childish venom. 'Oh, you've been with *her*.'

Alison stood immobile, steeling herself for a replay of the scene she had witnessed so often that she had lost count, but something went wrong with the familiar episode. Dirk disengaged himself calmly from Yvette's clinging arms and held her away from him.

'I think you'd better go home, Yvette. I want to be alone with my wife.'

'Your wife!' she snorted disdainfully, darting another venomous glance in Alison's direction. 'How can you still think of her as a *wife* after the way she walked out on you years ago without even telling you she was going to have your child?'

'Alison walked out under extreme provocation, and I was too blind to see that I was at fault,' Dirk's reply stilled the breath in Alison's throat. 'Now do as I suggest, Yvette. Go home and leave me alone with my wife.'

'You can't do this to me, you know!' Yvette shrieked, losing her composure so swiftly that Alison actually felt afraid for her. 'You can't treat me this way!'

'If you want to be made welcome in this house in future, then I suggest you do as you're told,' Dirk warned calmly but firmly, and Alison found herself blinking in astonishment as Yvette's faintly hysterical manner evaporated like mist before the sun.

'All right, I'll go,' she agreed petulantly, turning from them, but at the door she paused and glanced back at Dirk rather anxiously. 'You're not angry with me, are you?'

'No, I'm not angry with you.'

She nodded and walked out of the house, and moments later they heard that familiar roar of her Triumph as she drove away from the estate.

Alison felt confused and bewildered by the scene she had witnessed. From the depths of her subconscious an explanation for Yvette's behaviour fought its way to the forefront of her mind, but she thrust it aside and told herself that she was being ridiculous.

Dirk ushered her towards a chair, and she glanced up at him curiously as she lowered herself into it. 'You sent her away, and she went . . . almost like a child.'

'That's what she is—a child,' he confirmed, raking his fingers through his hair, and crossing the room to pour them each a lethal-looking drink.

'But she's . . . twenty-five?'

'Yes, she's twenty-five, but her reasoning, at times, is that of a child's,' Dirk confirmed the suspicions she had discarded as ridiculous. 'She suffered slight brain damage at birth. Her scholastic abilities were not affected, but it's left her unpredictable, impulsive, and childish in many ways.'

'I see,' Alison murmured with new understanding, accepting a drink from Dirk and sniffing at it to discover that it was brandy. It was not something she often drank, but in this instance she actually felt she needed it, and when the first fiery mouthful reached her stomach it slowly began to settle those quivering nerves.

Dirk did not sit down. He emptied his glass in two swift gulps, and placed it back on the cabinet to pace the floor restlessly. 'When my parents died they left

Bordeaux practically in ruins, and Yvette's father helped me get the estate back on to its feet, as it were,' he began to enlighten her for some reason, and she sat there quietly without interrupting him. 'I owe Cedric Paulson a debt of gratitude I could never repay entirely, and that's why I took it upon myself to help him with Yvette. For some obscure reason she seemed to have more confidence in me than in her father, and that's why I'm the one she runs to when she's in trouble, and the one whose advice she takes without a murmur. I can control her wayward behaviour and her childish tantrums, and I shall have to go on doing so until someone else comes along who can take over from me.'

What he did not say—perhaps because he was not aware of it—was that Yvette was in love with him, but Alison did not think this the right moment to enlighten him.

'Why didn't you tell me this before?' she asked quietly, understanding at last the odd relationship between her husband and this woman she had considered him to be in love with.

'Stubborn pride mostly,' came the harsh reply, then he paused directly in front of her and pinned her down with a steel-grey glance. 'When you care about someone you don't doubt them. That's what I thought, but I was wrong. Trust comes in time, through living together, and by openly discussing the things which might touch one.'

'I was young, too ... and foolish,' she conceded, lowering her gaze before the intensity of his.

'Perhaps,' he agreed, resuming his restless pacing. 'But I was older, and I should have had more sense. I should have known that a wife is not someone who simply accepts without question what her husband is doing, the way my mother used to do with my father.'

What was all this leading up to? What did it all mean? Did she dare nurture the hope that he cared, or would she simply be plunging herself deeper into the depths of despair?

'Did you know that I searched intensively for almost a year without finding you before I was forced to give up?' Dirk's voice intruded on her thoughts, and she looked up sharply.

'Why did you try to find me?'

'Why?' he laughed shortly and somewhat harshly. 'Because I realised soon enough what an idiot I'd been, and I wanted you back. When I couldn't find you I could only hope that you would come back to me some day of your own free will.'

That flame of hope was burning steadily now despite her efforts to douse it. 'Did you think I would come back after you'd delivered the ultimatum that, if I walked out, I wasn't to think I could come back to you again?'

'I hoped you would realise eventually that those words had been spoken in a moment of anger.'

Alison gazed up at him doubtfully. 'You weren't very pleased to see me that day at Solitaire.'

'Seeing you again was a shock that brought back the memory of those futile months I spent searching for you. I was angry with you as well as myself, but the unexpected discovery that I had a son sent my reasoning for a loop.' He gestured distastefully. 'I believed that all I wanted was revenge; revenge for all the suffering I'd endured, and revenge for not being told about Ferdie, but revenge has the sting of a scorpion when it recoils on one.'

Never, not since their first meeting, had they opened up so completely to each other, and Alison was not going to waste this opportunity. 'Did you think you were the only one who suffered?'

'Rational thinking has been beyond me these past months. I've been like Jekyll and Hyde; hating you, but wanting you. I used every little weapon that came my way to hurt you, and when I succeeded, I felt only disgust for myself.' Dirk flinched as if someone had struck him. 'God, Alison, you'll never know the hell I went through those months while I was trying to find you. You'd vanished so completely that I eventually found myself doing the rounds of the hospitals and mortuaries.'

They stared at each other across the space that divided them, and she longed to fling herself into his arms, but too much still had to be said. She took another steadying mouthful of brandy, and grimaced at the taste. She could not drink another drop, and, setting her glass aside, she rose to her feet to stare out of the window at the fine rain falling outside. The trees seemed to be shrouded in mist, or was it the mistiness of tears in her eyes?

'I had very little money with me when I arrived in Cape Town,' she began her recollections of that time after she had left Bordeaux. 'I had just enough, in fact, to pay for a few nights in an old lodging house, so I sold my car to the first buyer.'

'I traced your car, and followed the trail from there to the lodging house, but there the trail ended very mysteriously.'

'Jobs weren't so easy to get at the time, and I was getting desperate,' she continued, barely conscious that Dirk had spoken as she relived those incidents in her life. 'Dr Samuels finally took pity on me and found employment for me in a home for unmarried mothers, and this very conveniently included a room of my own on the premises. Ferdie was born there, and they were kind enough to let me stay on in a working capacity until I finally found myself more suitable employment with an engineering firm. Ferdie was old enough to go to a crèche at the time, and while he progressed from the crèche to nursery school, I worked myself up from typist to private secretary with one of the directors.'

'Alison . . .' Dirk spoke directly behind her, but she

was only vaguely aware of it as the misery of her existence continued to pour from her.

'It hasn't been easy living under a persistent cloud of guilt.' Stinging tears filled her eyes and momentarily blurred her vision, but she blinked them away. 'I should have told you I was pregnant, but it was the last straw as far as I was concerned when I came home that day and found you in the study with Yvette. I wanted to write to you after Ferdie was born, but I was afraid. I was afraid you would take me back for Ferdie's sake alone, and I couldn't—I didn't——'

'*Alison.*' His hands were heavy on her shoulders, burning her through the cotton of her blouse as he turned her slowly to face him, and there was no time to hide the fact that she had been crying as he tipped her face up to his. His eyes burned down into hers with a tender fire that seemed to consume her, and her pulse began to hammer wildly against her temples when his features softened in a bone-melting manner. 'I love you.'

Her heartbeat faltered, and raced on again at a most alarming pace as she stared up at him in stunned surprise. 'You—you've never said that to me before.'

'They're not words that come easy to a man who was raised on the belief that there's no such thing as love.' His hands gently framed her face and his thumbs lightly brushed away the tears on her cheeks. 'I think my parents hated each other's guts almost from the day they married until the day they died. I've often wondered why they married each other, but I guess I'll never know the answer.'

'Oh, Dirk,' she sighed, compassion mingling with the most indescribable joy as she went into his arms and clung to him as if she was afraid that this was no more than a dream.

His mouth found hers with a desperate hunger that matched her own, and she slipped her arms about his waist as she pressed her yielding softness into the hard curve of his body. She belonged at last, and the glowing warmth of happiness flooded her being.

'Small as you are, you're an incalculable force,' he smiled down at her when they finally paused to draw breath. 'You shattered my beliefs into fragments on that very first day we met when I found you standing so helplessly next to that contraption you had a nerve to call a car.'

Alison shook her head, her eyes luminous with the extent of her feelings. 'I—I can't believe it.'

'Believe it, Alison. My love for you is here.' Dirk took her hand and pressed it against his chest where she could feel the strong, hard beat of his heart beneath her fingers. 'Feel it, and learn to know it, because I can't promise that I shall say it often.'

Her eyes filled with tears as the last remaining doubt fled from her mind, and her tears glistened like pearls on her dark lashes when she smiled up at him. 'I love you, Dirk du Bois, and if you can't say it, then I'll say it for you. I love you with every beat of my heart, and with every breath that I take.'

She felt his chest heave beneath her hand before she was pulled almost roughly into his arms, and she raised her lips eagerly to meet his in a searing kiss that seemed to shake her to the very foundation of her soul. Desire mounted, sharp and sweet, but the next instant he dragged his lips from hers and buried his face in her fragrant hair.

'Oh, my God!' he groaned, his arms tightening almost convulsively about her waist until it felt as if her ribs would crack.

'What's wrong?' she whispered anxiously.

'I don't think I could ever explain to you how I felt when Kate telephoned me.' He shuddered against her and raised his tortured face to gaze down at her with that same wild look she had seen in his eyes when he had walked into Solitaire's living-room to find her sitting there. 'I thought you were dead.'